About the Author

Omar Sabbagh is a widely published prose and poetry writer, academic and Associate Professor of English at the American University in Dubai. *Minutes from the Miracle City* is his second novella.

D0309681

Minutes From The Miracle City

A tale of contemporary Dubai

OMAR SABBAGH

Fairlight Books

First published by Fairlight Books 2019

Fairlight Books
Summertown Pavilion, 18-24 Middle Way,
Oxford, OX2 7LG

A CIP catalogue record for this book is available from
the British Library

1 2 3 4 5 6 7 8 9 10

ISBN 978-1-912054-66-4

www.fairlightbooks.com

Printed and bound in Great Britain by Clays Ltd

Designed by Sara Wood
Illustrated by Sam Kalda
www.folioart.co.uk

MIX
Paper from
responsible sources
FSC
www.fsc.org
FSC® C018072

For Faten
My Storyteller

I

Hakim was like a ball of tickled childhood, as he waited for his mandarin-yellow sedan to rush over the bump in the road, a small blemish which had probably resulted from the pounding, garish heat. He always knew to expect it about twenty metres shy of the sign for exit 36.

As expected, the car made a small jiggle upwards as it rode at speed over the ungainly bump – and he was delighted. A wide thick-lipped grin spread across his road-riveted face. He was delighted, most of all, because it was a comfort, a deep comfort, to know that this bump in the highway, this unique fault and folly in the construction of the same, was made special by him, appreciating the glorious fluke of it; it seemed to make his workaday more his own somehow.

Hakim had been driving a taxi in Dubai for over twelve years. He'd watched the princedom grow. He'd seen it sprout towers, villas and compounds, schools and colleges, clinics and parks, restaurants and bars, hotels, banks, and roads and roads, and more and more roads and roads; all that, all this, until it made him dizzy to think of it. He'd seen the urban relish and gusto, the bravery and the brag and the boast of it all. And a small piece of his insides gloated to be a part, however slim, of that vision and tour de force – as though his soul's wide window was the more glint-ridden by dint of it, beneath the vast, electric, all-engulfing sun.

But these Englishmen, these Englishmen (for perhaps all westerners in Dubai were of a piece), all they knew was how to curse, disrespect and holler at all that was good and decent and halal. Yes, he now thought to himself, 'holler' was a good English word, and he'd bet his own brown and bearish soul that the present Englishman, screaming like an animal down his mobile while lodged in the backseat of Hakim's cab as they sped down the highway – he'd bet his own soul that this Englishman didn't himself know such a superb verb. 'Holler', yes. It probably came down from the word 'halal' itself!

'Listen mate. It's simple. Either they're able to get the thing built by the new year, or they can't. And if they can't the deal's off. We just don't have the bloody time or the money. And time is money…'

No, Hakim was thinking, money is time; money is time. Yes, that was the better conclusion to make. Not that this Englishman would ever understand the depth of that. Money was time. Hakim had nearly four full-grown children back

8

home in Pakistan. And wasn't it true that he'd sacrificed the last twelve years of his own life, a good and decent sum of time, to make the money that was necessary to give his beloved sons time to be better and get more than their father, grinding in this terrible, terrible heat?! And wouldn't – in the goodness of time, giving them the time of, and for, their more winning lives – wouldn't that lead to giving him time to relax and enjoy the autumn and the winter of his own life?

'Anyway,' the Englishman continued, rallying now to the close of his loud, adamant chinwag, 'I'll be in the office over the weekend, and we can crunch the numbers then... Yes, you have to come in on the weekend... I don't care if it's bloody Ramadan. You work for me. And God, well...' The Englishman paused for the first time in his heated call, then said, 'Doesn't it say somewhere in the Koran that God, that God... that God, I mean, helps those who help themselves? Something along those lines? Doesn't it?'

Oliver's chubby pink-white face seemed to slow in its fighting grimace. Business was business, of course, but he knew enough now of the princedom and its hale mores. So he didn't dare risk stepping on any toes, on any spiritual, soul-filled toes. He was a guest there, trying to ratchet-up a decent nest-egg – so spilt milk was not to be spilt. He needed and wanted to play by the rules, and fly under the radar just long enough to make some good and bulky brass! But his employees could be such whiners! He now wiped a tissue across his sweaty brow; his wife had packed a few in his jacket pocket earlier that morning. That was new; and, as it turned out, quite useful. Women were mercurial above all else, he knew that now in his marrow; but they were also, he now thought, quite practical.

Hakim could not decide whether he was or was not impressed. Of course, it did say something like that in the Holy Book. But was it for this '*In-gah-leesh*' to quote the word of God like this, as part of some business conversation? It was a worthy question. He made a mental note to cogitate on the matter later, after the end of his daylight shift, once he'd handed over his trusty sedan to his partner who drove the nights. Perhaps it might make a good topic of conversation at the *majlis*, over tea and roasted chestnuts? Perhaps; but then, perhaps not. Because there were better things to mull over and chat about with one's friends over a sumptuous, well-earned *Iftar*. Besides, Dubai was large and populous; though it had happened once or twice, as if willed by the hands of angels or *djinns*, Hakim was quite certain he'd never encounter this same customer-Englishman again.

*

As he stood now in a longish queue, thinking that he'd got all he needed for the evening repast, Hakim was nonetheless preoccupied with the recently soured relationship between himself and his partner, who drove the nights.

Vinod was a Hindu, so there shouldn't have been any tetchiness about working the night shift during Ramadan, for what did Ramadan mean to him? Yes, Vinod was Indian, but Hakim had had good relations with Indians before. He'd even had some buddies from India; not close friends, mind you, but still, he'd been on good terms with many an Indian, which made him, he now thought, quite the diplomat! A Pakistani peacemaker, that's what he was! He now pictured himself standing between the two leaders of the respective neighbouring nations of the Asian sub-continent, smiling gallantly, while facilitating an epic handshake for the world's media. CNN would be there, too, the great CNN, to capture him at his best, looking quite the statesman. He pictured his own elaborate dignity, and just as a smile began to vanquish his face, the checkout girl said:

'Forty-four dirhams and fifty.'

Hakim snapped out of his brimming reverie and dug his right hand into his righthand pocket. He spilled a couple of crumpled notes and a bunch of coins onto the counter, realising now that perhaps he'd overdone it with the shopping. The rice was a must, he wouldn't return that. The meat was a must, too. But the sardines, so nicely packed in their short pink and yellow, oval metal container, his treat to himself, well, they would have to go. And of course, the chewing gum. Muttering a few small blasphemies, he retreated, very much unlike a statesman, to replace the surplus goods. When he returned to pay the lesser sum, he couldn't but help feeling ashamed before the young Filipino who was chuckling with his colleague, while bagging his goods. Hakim felt angry, too. The whelp! Only a boy! Maybe twenty-five years of age at the most! And to laugh at his elder like that?! But then, perhaps sorrow, like his present sorrow, was the way of the world for the good, the hardworking, the honest, the brave. As he walked out of the grocery store, consoled, he felt once more like the statesman that he indubitably was.

That effortless melodrama enacted in the mind of the Pakistani customer who'd just left, walking with his head held hyperbolically high, donning the dignity of his wishes, was very, very far from the thoughts, chuckling or not, of the young Filipino in question. In fact, Ricardo had been laughing about something completely different, and had hardly noticed Hakim as a distinguished, or indeed distinguishable, individual. Bagging groceries all day long or trundling on his tricycle across the more affluent parts of Dubai in the viscid summer heat, the cloying summer humidity, to deliver the goods of the grocery store, he'd very little energy or need to take notice of each and every customer.

Ricardo was wearing faded blue jeans above his trusty white sneakers and the requisite uniform of light blue shirt with a small red triangular logo.

In the Philippines he had completed a Bachelor's degree in seamanship. But he'd left the maritime world quite soon after marriage and, as it happened, the pursuant pregnancy early on in his wedlock to Shirley; the resplendent Shirley! His love, his one and only. With a baby on the way, working in the Philippine navy, even as a chef, had not been an option. He could still hear his wife now, scolding him for getting her pregnant so soon after they'd wedded before God the Father, God the Son and God the Holy Spirit.

'You imbecile!' she'd exclaimed in their native tongue. She'd wide, thick lips, salmon-coloured, clown-shaped. Her mouth was mouthing the words like a carnival. 'You couldn't wait a few months?! You don't know your manly business! And now, now, we have to think what to do! You cannot leave me like this. You must think of a good plan. A good plan!'

And then, miming her own (fat) mother, Ricardo's dreaded in-law, she'd rapped him across the shoulder with a half-clasped fist, a kind of petulant grimace overwhelming her otherwise quite effortlessly beautiful face. When she clenched her teeth like that, she was most attractive. She was like an Amazonian woman. Ricardo had read of the Amazons while still at school, and their mythology had fascinated him. Their spears and shields. Their long tresses of dark brown wavy hair. Their arrows, their arrows.

After softly punching him, her face had begun to screw up with emotion. Ricardo knew better at the time than to protest. Instead he tried, by turns, a different tack. It really wasn't his fault, he'd insisted. She was 'just too sexy; just too sexy.' He'd grinned mock-heroically, thinking the compliment a timely, masterful stroke. And though he'd had one other ploy lying in wait – namely to place the blame in the capable lap of the Catholic God they both believed in – Shirley wasn't dim. No, he now thought, she was very, very far from dim; and that was good, because she made a good mother for his son, and that was bad, because it seemed like he could never get away with anything.

He thought of her short, bobbed glut of almond-russet hair, how silky it was and how lucky he was to have a wife with such a silken mane. Of course, that was to be expected, such a glamorous appearance; she was a beautician after all. She could out-manicure and out-pedicure all her colleagues: Filipino, Nepalese, Egyptian or from wherever, this he knew. She was trained in the beautifying arts like a white witch! In point of fact, her wages were larger than his own. And to add to that she had to take their child to work with her every day. It was lucky that she'd such an understanding boss – a Moroccan lady, Farah, whom he'd met only once, and was so unlike the few Moroccans he'd met over the last three years in Dubai. Because Farah, with her fake blond hair, her fake jewels bejewelling her fingers, her breast implants and Botox-lips – Farah was a godsend. When he'd met her, only once, she'd told him of her pleasure at Shirley's work ethic and the quality of her work.

'And the child, to bring the child here, as long as he doesn't make too much noise and disturb the clientele, that's fine; the child being here, I mean.' Farah's smile was ingratiating in a way that suggested immense dignity, more like an aristocrat than a beauty salon manager from Casablanca.

She was a good boss; Ricardo couldn't believe his, their, luck. And he'd said so, though Shirley had pinched him tersely behind his back, irritated beyond measure. But it was true: Farah was a godsend. She might look like a doll, but she'd the heart of an ox. Or a sealion, Ricardo now concluded. Yes, sealion was better.

There were no Moroccans in the Philippines. At least, as far as he knew. But perhaps there were? What any Moroccans might be doing there, he'd no idea. He now wondered if he should find out if there were Moroccans in the Philippines. Shirley's boss was a nice lady, and she might be gratified to hear of the fates of her compatriots in what to her was a distant land. He would ask his brother, Benedict.

Meanwhile, as he zoomed back to his workaday, he said to himself in a sibilant whisper that Shirley would be pleased. He'd made forty-three dirhams above his wages that day and was chuffed. Tips were always welcome. Tips were, in fact, a thing of beauty and a joy forever.

He'd heard that phrase, shouted sarcastically by an Englishman the other weekend, when he was out for the karaoke night with Shirley and their friends. It was poetry. And here, too, was 'poetry'.

He would ask Shirley what she thought of poetry. And if there were any good Philippine poets. Surely, there must be. He thought all this while packing the last set of bags for the last customer. The security guard, a black man from Uganda named Patrick, was preparing to shut up shop. Ricardo's relief turned his mind, happily, gleefully, back onto the extra cash now swimming – but dry and brittle, as befitted good paper currency – in his pocket. Two light leaf-green notes and one blue one; a few loose coins to boot.

When he'd made a small fortune like he had that day, money that would go straight into his savings for the toy dinosaur his three-year-old wanted for his upcoming birthday, he was more than open to ribaldry. His chum's recent jesting, a dose of braggadocio based on bachelor escapades the weekend preceding – the bantering laughter Hakim had so misunderstood as directed at him – had been welcome to Ricardo, in his new-found wealth. It was like his lungs inflated with the extra cash, making room for the more bellying laughter.

But the raucousness of the laughter reminded him, too, of how tired he was. His thyme-yellow skin looked almost as drained as it felt. He'd the usual long journey home by metro, both lines, urban and suburban, to look forward to, followed by the twenty-minute walk to his small one-bedroom apartment on the greener outskirts of this large and populous metropolis. And he was cursing himself for having left his earphones at home that morning, which meant he'd have to undergo the trip without the companionship of his beloved music. Without the Beatles in fact; but more sadly, without ABBA. Both he and Shirley and most of their friends adored ABBA; were devoted to them. Not a single song of theirs was off or weak. Ricardo sometimes wished he'd lived in the 1970s, so he might have attended ABBA in concert, as live as live can be. That would have been something! He would have been king of the Philippines had he seen them on stage, live. He would have garnered the envy of all his friends and family! No doubt, on recognising how devoted he was to their music, ABBA would have invited him backstage. No doubt, they would have offered a singalong session. But no: the hour-plus journey home would be packed only with the sound of the electric wheels cogging along. ABBA would be missed, deeply, deeply missed.

Presently, he dug his hand into his pocket and rustled the cash there. It gave him renewed courage. Shirley would be pleased; yes, Shirley would most definitely be pleased.

II

Patrick, the Ugandan security guard, was lolling on his day off in the small bohemian bistro-bar where his brother worked as a waiter. He wanted to speak to his brother about a very important matter but, presently, was unable to. Edouard trafficked with small white towers of laden plates and laden cups and saucers, the carousel of his workaday world, and had no time to stop and chat, except for now and then scolding his brother's idleness when passing within earshot. Sat in the far corner of the small Parisian-looking place, closest to the door onto the kitchen, Patrick spent the first hours of his brother's morning shift thinking of ways to break the news. Every so often his eyes would stretch towards the moving form of his elder sibling, as though to beseech him to stop and stay awhile, to listen. Even though it was he, Patrick, who was burdened with the news that needed telling, his eyes looked like watery question marks.

Unlike Edouard, who'd arrived in Dubai years before his younger brother, Patrick had stayed long enough in their native country to finish his Bachelor's degree in media studies. He wanted to work in journalism, desperately, but after all his optimism on arriving (degree certificate in tow) in Dubai, he was now working alternating shifts as a security guard at a grocery store. As luck would have it, sporty from youth, Patrick had the build of a boxer; he was also black, which spoke volumes even if it shouldn't have, and was able to convince the store manager of his open-palmed honesty. The job didn't satisfy him, of course, but it was easy work. He laughed in his head at the fact that however small his wages were, they were being paid him for a holiday. Everyone knew how safe and secure Dubai was. Even the nightclub bouncers were rarely stirred into fisticuffs of any sort, no matter how many raucous, beefy expats they encountered. That said, when the store was particularly busy, his pal Ricardo would ask him to help with the bagging of the goods. But that was no harm done, because Ricardo was a gentleman in Patrick's book. He'd a young family, and in character he was a very different sort from the other Filipino workers, who were mostly braggers of the sorriest order. All they could talk about were the women they'd tried to screw or had succeeded in doing so. It was true, Patrick missed Africa, but one had to get on with life because it was to be lived, and lived only once. The world of media awaited him – with open arms no doubt, once the right people knew of his multifarious skills and the dedication he harboured. He dreamt of one day being an anchor on the BBC.

Seated together during the brief respite of his brother's lunch break, Patrick tried to broach the subject. However, nothing but inconsequential verbiage came out, like a blocking wall, stoppering the urgency that seemed to seep from his slightly sweaty dark skin. Edouard sensed something of the sort, and said:

'Listen. If you've something on your mind, spill it. I have to get back to work in twenty. And if you haven't, then stop this fidgeting. Why are you so nervy today? Something happen at work? You get fired or something? Because if you did, I can't help you. You'll have to pick yourself up; Mother is not here, you know, and Father is probably turning in his grave, debating with the worms and ants over who's got it worse.'

Patrick seemed to be honing the energy of his soul into his mouth. His nerves were on fire. His lips quivered, then he said:

'I don't know how to put this, so here it comes, as it truly is.'

'Tell me. You know you can tell me anything.' Edouard wiped some cappuccino cream from the rim of his upper lip. He continued to eye his brother, solicitously.

'I've written a book.'

'Excuse me?'

'I said: I've written this book.'

Edouard, tongue-tied, was trying to figure out which was the more perplexing, his brother supposedly having gone ahead and written a book, or the fact that he'd found it a difficult confession to make. What was so nerve-wracking in having written a book? If true, it was actually quite impressive. He screwed up his eyes, peering at his brother. It was an old scenario between the two of them; the older man the sceptic, the younger the epicurean.

'And... this is a problem: why?'

'Well, I've decided I want it to be published.'

'Naturally. So, go ahead. I still don't understand.'

'It's going to cost, that's the catch.'

Edouard smiled now, knowingly, while shaking his head like a wiseacre.

'I'm not asking for much. I just need you to lend me four thousand dirhams. That's the down payment with this publisher. The rest I'll pay, month by month, from my wages. Of course, it will mean I'll have to sacrifice many things, but it's a good book, and I want it to be read by the world. It will be such a success that we'll both have more money. And it will be my gateway into the media. CNN would never turn down a reporter who has published a book. Not a book like this!'

'The Ides of March.'

'What's that?'

'The Ides of March. Don't you remember? Father used to say it, whenever any of us children were stubborn or proud or just wanted what we couldn't have.'

'No, I don't. And Father is gone. It's just us now. And Mother.'

'Don't be a fool, Patrick. By all means write books. No one's saying you shouldn't. But don't waste money you just don't have! You owe it to yourself.' There was something almost plaintively maternal in Edouard's tone of voice.

Frustrated, Patrick curled his lips and hissed through his teeth. He knew he should have broached the subject in a subtler, more advantageous way; or, at a more propitious time. He'd predicted this. His brother's refusal, though, hadn't dampened the excitement he felt inside, like a child cosseting a newly bought toy.

The brothers soon went their separate ways, tacitly acknowledging, with a swift-handed, barren-eyed handshake, they'd meet up again the following week.

*

On the metro ride home later that day, Patrick was lost in thought. He and his brother were very different in temperament. While he was setting out to conquer as much of the world as he might grasp, Edouard was far more placid in his outlook on this life that had to be lived, and that had to be lived only once. If Edouard was given, say, only ten per cent of anything in life, he might say to himself that that was grand, grand indeed, because ten per cent was more than two. It wasn't necessarily that Patrick was more ambitious, because though in fact he was, he knew perfectly well that ambition could be a folly; no, it was his worldview. In the continuous game of gauging themselves against their wishes, present against past and against in-wending futures – a habit instilled in them from their mother, both brothers being the apples of her eyes – Edouard never failed to compare the positives with the wailing negatives that existed throughout most of the world. Patrick had always thought that such absolutism was simply a kind of ascetic, saintly madness! Each and every person had his or her own context; each and every moment was, like an atom, there to be split, and the explosion into newer, richer life was to be savoured to the draining of the last dreg! Patrick knew himself, and that he wished for risk, because for him risk was the very tenor of living. Edouard always sought out the kind of ease and comfort that was the normal territory of the more religious-minded, though, he practised no religion.

Then he remembered once more that thick sheaf of plumed manuscript back at his studio apartment in Bur Dubai; and his eyes were singing. He could see its ruffled crumpled sides, and the coffee stain on the front cover. He felt elated; strangely so, perhaps, since the way their meeting had gone, Edouard was unlikely now to loan him the money for the down payment. He felt elated, though, nonetheless. The prospect of seeing his book in print one day was far too powerful to be dimmed by a mere hiccup like that. He'd find a way.

'By hook or by crook,' as their mother used to say.

'But you do not see my point, sir. You simply do not see the wisdom, the depth of it!'

Patrick jolted upwards from his reverie. The small outburst was from an older, brown-skinned man further along the metro carriage, aimed at another brown-skinned man sitting opposite him. Patrick tried to close his eyes, to return to the phantasms of his waking slumber, but the small contretemps continued. And he couldn't help but overhear.

'He was right, don't you see? He was absolutely right!'

The man opposite Hakim mumbled something grumpily, saw that Hakim was about to launch into another tirade, then mumbled something else, but this time with a conciliatory air. Hakim clenched his lips, huffed, crossed his arms against his chest, and adamantly turned his neck to stare at the fading landscape of Dubai's suburbs swishing by, while listening to the chugging sound of the train. Their argument was closed.

Hakim had spent the last twenty minutes dilating on a small anecdote which he thought held eons and eras of wisdom within itself.

He was told of a shoe-shiner, a beggar almost, hailing from some small rustic village back home. Every morning this shoe-shiner woke up like clockwork, made his ablutions, drank some tea, munched a small morsel of bread and headed off to his stall near the marketplace of the city to which he'd moved at a young age. He would shine shoes for any of the more gentrified people who frequented that city, or for the (moneyed) tourists who sometimes sojourned there. In any case, this man would work from early morning until noonish, usually, and had done so from his youth into his now grizzled and grey middle age. He would make enough to satisfy his staple daily needs of shelter and nourishment; and then, sage as he was, any customer approaching for a shoeshine after that point was politely but resolutely rejected. He'd always done this; he still did, apparently. No, instead of making even a small amount more, this pauper-like chap would relay the customer to the next stall a kilometre away. He'd made enough money to live happily to the next day. And, in Hakim's view, it was this man, this man from the world-entire, who was the happiest man on Earth!

'Because he was at one with his environment. Therefore, he was at one with himself, too. Don't you see? He was a happier man than all of us.'

'Nonsense. Plain nonsense!' the other man had retorted, once Hakim had finished relating the morality tale.

Looking at Hakim, who, in turn, was staring glumly out of the window, like a sulking child, Patrick thought to himself that it took all sorts to make a world – which was a cliché. But clichés became so for a reason. He proceeded now, with much self-congratulation and ceremony, to dub himself 'a reflective conservative', miming a phrase one of his professors back in Uganda had once used, explaining his accepting, realistic outlook on life. It meant that he didn't over-question his everyday situations or surroundings, and thus didn't risk what had in fact happened in this professor's youth for too long; namely, undermining the very possibility of living that life! It sounded very sophisticated to Patrick's ear, and would no doubt find its way into one of his books one day.

III

The doorbell rang. While still busied by her phone conversation, Rachel got up from the tan leather couch of the living room and made her way to the door. She smiled to the Filipino young man, gesturing for him to carry the bags inside to the kitchen. She could do this with such ease and aplomb because he'd provided this service countless times over the last couple of years or so. While still busy with her chinwag, she pointed for Ricardo to also place one of the large two-gallon water-dispenser bottles inside the machine, smiling at him warmly, while still maintaining concentration on her conversation. It was a chequered performance, but the woman of the house was used to such multi-tasking.

Ricardo was always thrilled to deliver to this address. The Madam of the house always tipped well, and was always kind and respectful in other ways, quite unlike some of the English he delivered to; but it was also a pleasure for him to ogle the svelte luxury of their penthouse apartment, so close to the business hub of Dubai.

As you walked in, the kitchen was through a door on your left. But Ricardo had seen more of the place because on more than one occasion he'd been engaged in conversation with the Madam of the house, mere polite trifles, but still something of a trophy for the young Filipino. Through the hallway, past the kitchen door on the left and the bedroom door on the right, there was open-planned space where a mahogany dining table and plush extended salon formed one long curving oblong shape, with two windows opening onto balconies pitting the far wall. The walls were painted in a colour somewhere between violet and a silvery grey, and these chilling colours, along with the expensive-looking paintings, cooled the mind as much as the pulsing AC did the body.

Ricardo dreamt of one day owning an apartment like this; or maybe half like this; or maybe just a quarter? It was almost guaranteed never ever to happen; he was sane and honest enough with himself to know that. But it pleased him to think of his Shirley being made a woman of leisure like this kind Madam. It was true that, together, he and his wife made more money and lived a better lifestyle in Dubai than they would ever have managed back home. But there was always room for daydreaming of living like this! Imagine it! Just imagine! To live like kings and queens! Like hapless clowns in a universe of workers! But then, no, he thought, the Sir of the house, whom he'd only seen twice, must work himself to make the money to live like this. So, no, not clowns in the universe. More like masters of ceremonies. Better. Ricardo had always loved the circus, or at least the notion of one, never having been to one. He'd read of it in a book during his schooldays.

He now greeted the girl-child of the house, politely and with gallant deference. A four-year-old, close in size to his own child, she'd just sauntered into the kitchen, clasping her teddy bear and presently tugging at her mother's trousers, for attention. What he would give for his son one day to grow into such luxury, such comfort and wealth! True, he again conceded to himself, he most probably would never be able to give Shirley a life like this – but his son? Who knew where destiny would take him? His daydreaming was inflamed as he helped the nanny-cum-maid to unload the goods which he'd just set on the kitchen counter. Rachel McGinn was trying to keep up with her friend on the phone, who was narrating an anecdote about her husband.

Sakina and Rami were a Lebanese couple based in Dubai whom they'd got to know through the mutual business interests Rami had with her husband, Oliver. Rachel continued to listen to the tale, while still pointing her fingers frantically for Lakshmy, the Nepalese nanny-cum-maid, and Ricardo to place the goods in their due, respective places. It was a hectic process, and while doing all this, she stroked her daughter's long blond hair, which seemed to soothe her.

Sakina was saying how a few weeks earlier Rami had been traipsing through 'the monstrosity' that was the Dubai Mall, and how at one point his wedding ring had slipped off his finger. She was giggling nervously as she told the story, because she wasn't quite sure how she felt about it all.

He had only realised it was missing when he arrived back home later that day, which was typical of Rami. He hadn't told her at the time. And, fearing 'wifely wrath', as he'd put it (to Sakina's delight or anger, she wasn't quite sure) he had phoned up the security or whatever relevant office at the Mall was responsible for such things, telling of his mishap. He asked, naturally, for them to check the 'Lost and Found'. And they duly found no ring waiting. So, they called him in, needing his presence to help. At this point, Sakina paused in her retelling, on the cusp of the marvel.

Rami said he entered a room, well-nigh a half-mile long, walled from wall to wall with surveillance cameras.

'It was a humungous space, and his breath literally stopped in his throat when he entered,' Sakina continued.

So, they asked Rami when and where he might have lost his ring. He made various calculations and was able to narrow the time and place he may have lost it to a workable hypothesis. After trawling through hyper-detailed videos, they finally found where he had dropped the ring, and saw what happened next. The camera in question picked up the image of a youngish man who bent down in the area in question, picked up the ring, took a quick look around him to make sure nobody was watching, and pocketed it. Unfortunately for him, as he turned to walk away, the camera had caught a glimpse of his face. And miraculously, the security officer in question was able to use this image to shuffle through a highly sophisticated network of identifying images.

'So anyway, they found the guy, and where he worked,' Sakina was saying.

As it happened the man in question wasn't employed at that Mall but was there merely as part of some service to one of the retail outlets there. His place of work made known, security immediately called up the company and had the man brought in. Now caught, he had handed over the ring, glum and shamefaced.

'And all this happened within a few hours of his calling in, can you believe it?!'

Surprised as Rami was at this resolution, when asked if he'd like to press charges, he had demurred.

'Rami said that the guy was so unhappy, looked so crestfallen, that he didn't have the heart. You know Rami, he's so soft-hearted.'

All the groceries had now been dispatched to their rightful places. Ricardo was standing at the entrance of the kitchen, feeling a little foolish. A minute later, having wrapped up the conversation by feigning gratuitous incredulity at the fortunate outcome, Mrs McGinn put her mobile down, slapped her forehead in deprecation and said:

'I'm so sorry Rick. I forgot I need to pay. How much is it?'

Ricardo handed her the bill. She quickly searched her pockets, then asked Lakshmy with urgency to get her purse from her handbag. It was in the bedroom, next to her side of the bed. Meanwhile, she engaged Ricardo, asking after Shirley and their little one.

'Oh! A toy dinosaur! Did you hear that, Olivia?'

The small girl nodded her head obediently, still clinging to the side of her mother's trousers, smiling sweetly at her mother and then at Ricardo, back and forth.

Rachel paid the bill, and then paused to search for a few extra notes. Ricardo uttered a wide array of obsequious pleasantries, accepting the twenty-dirham tip with his usual clowning grace. As he left, he asked God the Father and God the Son and God the Holy Spirit to bless the family residing in that penthouse at the top of a bluey-silver tower close to Dubai's financial district.

On moving to this apartment Rachel had planted a writing desk at the far end of the long curving open-planned living area, a small out-fitted space facing the awesome view over Dubai on which her laptop now lay, opened for work. After giving Olivia a lollipop from the kitchen cabinet, the one with all the naughty 'goodies' in it, and having Lakshmy take her daughter back to her playroom, Rachel returned to the desk to try and get on with the work she'd planned for the day. Sakina's call had interrupted her; then Ricardo had intervened, too. Both were necessary interruptions. But perhaps now she might get some writing done?!

Before marrying Oliver, she'd worked for a good decade as a journalist. Since then she'd tried to keep up with it, even in Dubai. It was a matter of self-esteem in the main, the money being of only secondary importance. For the first two years she'd been able to shift her job to the Dubai office. But then Olivia began to get bigger, and more of a handful, and Oliver's business seemed to be doing, well, it actually was doing much better, after the 2008 financial fiasco. So, for the last year or so, a newly made housewife (though she preferred the term 'homemaker'), she'd made a pact with herself that she'd try her hand at writing fiction, a long and for so long forlorn dream she'd had since her teenage years. She wanted to write novels that could make use of her knowledge of the region's politics she had covered for so long. Yes, Middle Eastern politics could be incorrigibly Byzantine, but that only suggested to her that some tale making use of what she knew of the region might be the more thrilling and compelling for it. Above the writing desk were a few bookshelves, on which she'd placed the collected works of one of her favourite authors, John le Carré. She dreamt of being able to write a novel only half as good as that great man. Supposedly, she'd the time now to do it.

Her husband had always said that 'time was money.' That hackneyed phrase remained like a talisman between them from the first night they met, having been set up by two mutual friends. He'd arrived late to their first date. And when she'd shyly indicated her disappointment, out came the phrase.

'Well, yes, you are right. Time is money I always say.' He was wearing black jeans and a black shirt. He was quite skinny in those days. And they'd had chemistry from the start. He was surprisingly good with words, for a businessman. Though he had said he wasn't much interested in politics, he was a good listener, and pretended at least to be interested in her views over those first few dates. They were both headstrong people, but they also found over the first year of their relationship that they complemented each other. Though thoroughly business-minded, Oliver just wasn't practical when it came to the minutiae of his everyday routine. And though she was admittedly obsessive-compulsive when it came to organisation, she had learnt to mellow over the years. He became more well turned out, and she less highly strung. God! All those years ago!

She could still remember their first kiss, which came at the end of that first date, and how it was sealed by the phrase in question. He was saying good night, and then, looking deep into her eyes, he said, leaning forward gently, slowly:

'Time is money. That means I owe you.'

And then bending in for the kill, such a smelting kill, he'd kissed her. It was, no question, a smooth move. She'd asked for the 'interest' on the loan. And he'd kissed her again.

Time is money. Though it was his motto, she knew he didn't really mean anything so callous, now as then. It was just business-minded bravado. Besides, the opposite was in fact just as true. She had, supposedly at least, more time now to work on her own writing, precisely because of his financial and business success over the last five years or so. Money was time, then.

All that said, she was still undecided about Dubai as a place to bring up their daughter, Olivia. Yes, it was stable, it was safe, and by all the portents quite nicely geared for young families. But still, years on, she wasn't quite sure. Did she want Olivia to grow up in the Middle East, however glamorous their lifestyle? Would she think of England as a foreign place? Would she think, like so many of the well-off couples in their milieu, that all the mainly Asian working class were somehow sub-human, there merely to serve? She worried about such things, but only rarely spoke to Oliver about them. She knew if she did, for all his loving care, he'd brush them aside as useless worry. He was a kind-hearted man, and quite understanding about most things. But time was money, for the time being at least.

It was now close to seven in the evening, and the summer sky was beginning to mellow into lavender and gunmetal, reflecting in mellifluous glints off the serried array of towers peppering the skyline. When she opened her laptop once more, however, she read through recent emails. Presently, she recalled a message from a day or two earlier which she'd neglected to attend to. It was from an old colleague, an Emirati journalist who'd grown up in Dubai, but whom she'd first known in London, and who had by chance happened to return to his homeland close to the time she had moved there with her husband.

She'd always loved Saeed, for his earnestness above all else. He wasn't your staple hack. No, he was a real, bona fide intellectual who read widely in more than three languages, and she was delighted to hear from him. It had been a while; Dubai did that to friendships. It was like the gigantic highways that separated everyday venues from each other by vast distances, which were mirrored by the distances between friends meaning that you had to be proactive in keeping the relationship going. Everyone in Dubai had their own bubble to grapple with. Of course, she'd also been so busy with Olivia; and Saeed, she presumed, had been busy with his career.

It seemed he wanted to meet with her – to talk shop, as well as just wanting to see her, his old friend. She remembered so well so many of their conversations in London, over lunch in the Starbucks of the building in which they both worked. His talk caterwauled all over the place, but with real cogency and coherence. He had always been such an insightful man. In fact, she'd always thought he should have been an academic, not a journalist. He was a manqué scholar. But then, perhaps in the world's current climate, a deeper, more-serious-minded journalist was just what was needed.

It seemed that he, too, was working on a book, whose title was *Minutes from the Miracle City*. It was to be a prolonged meditation on the phenomenon of contemporary Dubai. She reread the email again now…

Dear Rachel,

It's been a while, I know. I do hope that all is well your end? And that your husband and lovely daughter are in good health and in good spirits! I'm writing here because I miss you, and the long, epic chats we were wont to have. You were always one of the few colleagues and friends I've ever had who unfailingly

understood me, and the direction of my work.
Perhaps we might meet soon, tomorrow if at all
possible. It'll be more difficult, you see, to meet
during Eid or close after. I'd like to pick your
brain, about a series of articles I'm currently in
the process of writing. In fact, I hope to make
this series into a book eventually. Because I
truly feel like certain ideas and experiences
are now crystallising in the most fertile way. I
feel, in short, that it's time I made my mark,
irrevocably. Perhaps, if you're able to find the
time, we might meet. Tomorrow even? Please
do let me know. As I say, you are much missed!

With warmest wishes, your old friend,
Saeed

Finishing her second quick perusal of the email,
her mobile now trilled, then tinkled. It was Oliver.
He would be staying late at work. She sighed.
Time was money again.

She looked in at the open doorway to make
sure Olivia was tucked up, deep in sleep. Then she
poked her head in at Lakshmy's door.

'Sir is coming late tonight.'

Lakshmy smiled a beaming yet placid smile. She
always gave the impression of being unperturbed
by the topsy-turvy universe.

'Yes, Madam. There is food waiting, prepared, in
the microwave.'

Just as Rachel was about to go to the master bedroom, to take a shower and freshen up for bed, she opened her mouth to say something. A question rustled through her mind, something like: 'Lakshmy? Are you happy here? And not only here, but in your life?' However, she said no such thing. She only said:

'Well, good night then.'

'Good night, Madam.'

IV

Because his younger sister's car was at the garage, undergoing certain repairs, it fell to Saeed to have to go out of his way to pick her up from the beauty salon. She'd said she wanted to do a full makeover for the upcoming Eid and Eid-break following, which had of course quite pleased Lamise, their mother.

A thick set woman with a still-handsome face, the mother in question had just yelled from her bedroom for Saeed to set off now to fetch Hala. Saeed's elder sister Maryam, who lived next door in a simple two-storey villa equally forged of seamless camel-coloured stone, was nowhere to be seen. She'd got in the habit recently of absconding most afternoons with her little boy, Walid, and no one in the neighbouring household had been able to wangle it out of her where she went each day. Maryam's husband didn't seem to notice or mind; he was always preoccupied with his ailing business affairs in any case. But it was a nuisance, because at times like this it was Saeed who was called upon to be the chauffeur, the fixer, the handyman. It irked him, because he felt he had too much work on his mind of late that needed seeing to; there were always books to read, thoughts to think, texts to write.

And then there was the question of the other kind of love he harboured like bait, hope? He liked to think of his amatory independence as somehow noble or ennobling. But somewhere deep inside he knew that that was a cop-out. He was getting on in age, and however much his mother might press on the subject, and however much he might demur, she was probably right; it was about time. But then, who? And where? And how? The wheel of fortune hadn't been propitious as yet. But then again, yes, you had to bet on a number or two if you wanted to have hopes of the ball landing your fortune. And he berated himself for not having rolled the dice – to mix the gambling metaphor. He was aging; yes, that was certain.

His mother was now sixty-four years old. Their father had died only five years earlier, at the age of sixty-nine. In fact, it was his father's passing that had mainly triggered Saeed's return to Dubai, his homeland and still very much the love of his life. To date at least.

Though he'd grown up and pursued his preliminary studies in Dubai, at a time when the metropolis looked far different and far sparser than it did at present, he'd travelled to the UK to pursue his graduate studies, and on completion had landed his first full-time role in journalism there. He'd thrilled of course to the liberal and civil mores of the West, despite the tender spot, infinitely vulnerable, he harboured in his heart for Dubai. His experience abroad had opened his eyes and opened his heart. And now Hala, too, was on the cusp of pursuing her Masters. She wanted to travel to the UK, imitating her brother, but their mother would certainly not allow it. While not forbidding her youngest from pursuing her studies – though what Hala needed another degree for was beyond her – their mother could not allow her to travel so far away on her own; no, not a young girl as ludicrously beautiful as her. That said, when Saeed spoke of his London days, he could tell his mother secretly found it intriguing, this place continents away where her beloved boy had spent so much of the prime of his life. Surreptitiously taking advantage of this curiosity, Saeed was still in the process of trying to win over his mother to the idea of letting Hala study in the UK. She'd been accepted by two very good universities there, but their mother was still adamant, and Saeed didn't see the need to sour things overly. Besides, that was still months away; there was still time.

'I understand,' their mother would say, 'you think London glamorous, better than here. It is not. Yes, Saeed, you are a man, and your father and I were glad, very glad, to let you explore this world of ours. But Hala going there? No. You are the man of the family now, and you must think about your sister's future, all of our futures, with more responsibility.'

And knowing his mother like the back of his hand, Saeed would kowtow. The prime source of his mother's reluctance wasn't just conventional worry; that was purely a façade. It was, deep down, because her sister's daughter, his own cousin, had gone only five years earlier to study medicine in the US, and had never come back. It had been a harrowing time for his aunt; and thanks to this, his mother was petrified at the thought of a repetition of that fiasco. He and Hala, though, were still in cahoots, plotting and politicking. Aside from the actual material endeavour of getting their mother's blessing, they enjoyed such conspiratorial intrigue, being as siblings like two peas in a pod. For Saeed was closer in character and inclination to his younger sister, both displaying a highly intellectual bent.

Maryam, their elder sister, was more traditional. She'd married late, at the ripe old age of thirty. Their mother had almost given up, despaired. It wasn't that Maryam was stubborn, like her youngest sibling (that girl was just asking for trouble!). It was perhaps because Maryam wasn't the most beautiful of women. Knowing this herself, the older she got as a single woman, the more self-conscious and awkward she'd become; and, thus, the less likely to snag a husband. Her eventual husband Akram, though a good deal older, had been able and willing to see through Maryam's gauche ways, and, himself marrying very late, they'd come to what was evidently a working understanding. The matriarch of the family had rejoiced, praising the Deity in hitherto unsung hyperbole. And in any case, now with her young grandson only next door, bygones were indeed bygones. 'Better later than never,' Saeed had quipped at the time to tease his mother, while visiting Dubai briefly to attend the wedding. His mother had glared at her son with lightsome venom, which he knew to mean two things: first, don't make light of such a godly and heaven-sent thing as marriage; second, you yourself should get a move on and marry! And yet, despite that poisonous glare from his mother, the mispronounced English phrase had remained with her, she whose English was very limited, though more fluent perhaps than mere pidgin.

Maryam's boy Walid was the joy in the lives of both women, mother and grandmother. And both women were planning to take him shopping in the next day or two, to buy him new shoes and a new outfit in which to celebrate the upcoming Eid. Walid, at eleven-and-a-half years of age, was cognisant enough to feign interest in the new clothes and the long, boring trek round the Mall, in order not to dampen the good prospects he had of his other Eid presents (money, hopefully) from his grandmother and his uncle and aunt. Hala, still in her mid-twenties, and of course still unmarried, had always been closer to a big sister to Walid, than an aunt. And Walid revered his uncle Saeed, though for whatever reason he was still unconscionably shy in his presence.

Saeed's mother now yelled again from her bedroom:

'Saeed! Saeed! You must go now! She will be finished in ten minutes. She just called. And don't forget: it's a women's only salon!'

But forget he did.

Two full strides into the salon, with a mild and plaintive look on his face, a striking woman of close to his own age barred his way, with a grimace, while beginning to scold him. A Greek-type looking a bit like Sophia Loren, she was wearing all black, and her chestnut hair was bobbed up like a bird's nest on her crown. She was, he had to admit, striking.

'Excuse me! Excuse me! Only women allowed here! Only women!'

Taken aback, embarrassed, Saeed couldn't help his grin, filled with boyish charm and mischief. Quickly, as though to tease the woman, he went on tiptoes and peered over Farida's shoulder, spotting Hala seated at the far end of the salon being treated by a short, squat but also quite beautiful Filipino woman. Hala waved vigorously, gleefully, upsetting by the way Shirley's right hand as she was trying to pin a clasp in her client's hair.

The salon manager, Farah, now came over, her bangles jingling. She tried to alleviate the situation which was being stirred up between her Moroccan compatriot and employee Farida, and this handsome, intelligent-looking gentleman who was, it seemed, Hala's older brother.

Farah eased him out of the salon, and Saeed shouted mirthfully as he was being shuffled out that he'd wait for Hala in the car. Farida went back to her own client, visibly ruffled by the intrusion. While recommencing her spraying of the hairdo beneath her magical fingers, she turned to her right and addressed Shirley.

'That's the second time that's happened this week. What's so difficult about a women's only salon, in Dubai of all places!? I mean, don't they get it, from the closed, windowless door? And now of all times, so close to Eid.'

Shirley was putting the finishing touches on Hala's hair. She showed her the nearly finished makeover in the handheld mirror, to complement the one on the wall facing them. Hala smiled briskly at the mirror and at Shirley, too, because the two women were friends. Whenever she came to this salon, Shirley would confide in Hala like she did to no one else, except that is for Farida. Once, thinking herself pregnant again, she'd wept over Hala's shoulder. Another time, thinking

49

she'd got cancer, she'd done the same. Incorrigibly emotional, Hala adored the Philippine beautician. And though she'd not the same intimacy with Farida, especially given the distance in age, the two women respected each other, also with affection.

Hala now said, proceeding to ignore her looks in the mirror:

'Farida, my dear, you must understand that my brother is a "great intellectual", and that he has studied in the UK and worked there for many years. Yes,' she continued, caustically, 'he is a very, a very important person.' Her sarcastic smile brought out her dimples and her nostrils flared slightly, momentarily.

Farida huffed, pursed her lips in conciliation, and waved the air as if to say that bygones were bygones.

'For you, my life, I'll forgive him.' Then Shirley said:

'Your brother is a very handsome man; is he married?'

Hala thanked Shirley for the vicarious compliment, exuding her habitual chirpy grace. 'No,' she said. And it was a tart topic in her own mind. She loved her brother of course, immensely; and loved him to boot very much as his own man, independent to a certain extent at least of some of the staple traditions of the Gulf. But for all her own liberality and progressiveness, she still couldn't help but harbour a potent wish to see her older brother married and in love and procreating out of that love.

She now turned again to Farida, and said:

'You mustn't be harsh on men, you know. Without them none of us would be here.'

Farida thought this trivial, glib. And she said so, with mock-ire, teasing the younger woman. She was an innocent and merited all the protectiveness a woman like Farida could muster, after losing so much of her own in the strife that had been her life, landing there in Dubai at the calmed tail-end of it. She uttered a few curt maternal words to Hala, scattering her vexation in the warmth of their friendship.

Now in her mid-thirties, Farida had been married once; and divorced once. When still an adolescent she hadn't so much been forced, as subtly coerced into an arranged marriage. The second cousin in question had been, during their very brief courtship, the picture of attentiveness, and at nineteen Farida had been an innocent, much like Hala, she now thought. She knew far too little of men, though, and the dire vagaries of relationships. Ideally, before they'd married, they should have lived together for six months, say. But that possibility was none such, not in Morocco, not for a young and dutiful Muslim woman. And close to six months into their marriage, Mustafa, her husband became a changed man.

A nineteen-year-old bride was expected to bear children forthwith! They'd tried, of course, tried and tried again, but nothing gained. Farida's mother and mother-in-law waylaid her with potions and other forms of herbal witchery, assured as they were of such customary resorts, aimed at eliciting a newborn. And yet, after six months, being duly tested, if in secret, it turned out that Mustafa was wholly infertile. His own mother couldn't and wouldn't countenance the fact. So, she'd made Farida's life an increasingly hellish inferno.

Mustafa had prided himself on his liberality and his dynamism. He played five or six sports, regularly. But now he took it further, and for all the wrong reasons; he began to drink, smoke. And though it was he who'd told her to take off the hijab, which was the traditional headwear for a practising Muslim woman, her life became a misery for the year and a half they were married. Beforehand, Mustafa had seemed such a happy-go-lucky young man, and even if she'd not been in love, not by any means, she'd envisioned how she might come to love him in time. But then, once married, he turned into a jealous monster. He wouldn't let her go out with the few friends she had. He limited the number of guests she might want to invite to their small house. And when they went out, dancing even, he guarded her with such uptight jealousy it made her feel like a prisoner. It was more like martial discipline than a loving relationship.

Thankfully, she'd managed to get the divorce before it was too late. A good and talented lawyer friend of her elder brother's had weighed in. But a divorcée at the age of twenty-one in her milieu and familial surroundings was a burden, financially and otherwise; and she'd felt it, like a stigma. It was then that the idea kindled that she needed to move, for a new start and a different life. Thus and so, a few years later, having saved as much as she could, she'd taken her route to Dubai, to find her way and, perhaps, her fortune. And ever since, Farida was adamant she wouldn't make the same mistake again and become beholden to a man. She now said, quelling her defences after the recent intrusion:

'And you, my lovely? When are you going to settle down?'

'Oh, that. No, not for a while yet. I hope to go to the UK after summer. I want to do my Masters there.'

Farida smiled across at her again, with maternal warmth.

So, the three women, all so different, all so alike, continued talking for the next ten minutes while Saeed waited in the car. Hala regaled them, no longer poking loving fun at him, with tales of his intellectual curiosity and heroism. How he could talk and talk well, in a way that opened vast horizons, on nearly every subject. How he'd read maybe more than five thousand books and retained the content of at least half of them. How he'd studied and lived in London, like she wished to. How in short, he was the epitome of a man of the world.

That said, though, he was indeed a man of the world, he wasn't worldly. He didn't covet material things: a fancy car, fancy clothes. His kicks he got from more symbolic concerns, which she thought still more noble. He'd once told her, admitted almost, that his hunger for recognition in and for his work was no more noble than wanting a Ferrari. But she had protested at his modesty. Revering, idolising him, and herself wanting to progress in the worlds of the intellect, she held fast to the idea that mental pursuits were of a different qualitative tenor to material ones. 'Higher and lower pleasures,' she'd said to him once (trying to show off her latest readerly discovery) – as John Stuart Mill had theorised; adapting, tweaking and improving the utilitarian theory from its Benthamite facility! And then they'd had a discussion about desire; yet another of their epic, intellectual chinwags.

Saeed had spoken of Freud and his theory of 'the displacement of the object.' Because humans were the only animal that not only needed things such as nourishment, but also wished for them at the same time, and because there was always going to be a disjunct between these two impulses, the grass, as it were, was always greener elsewhere, beyond. The first objective need for the infant was milk, he'd said. But unlike the rest of the animal kingdom, when that human infant went towards that need instinctually, at the same time, they in effect said to themselves, 'I like this, I want this.' What this meant, Saeed had continued, was that you saved up for the Ferrari, but within a year, you wanted the private plane, and the next thing, and the next thing, namely, a condo on Mars, and so on. And unlike the angels, too, he'd said, who were also at one with their environment. Other animals wished what they needed, and needed what they wished, and angels were already at one with God. God! Her brother could talk!

When they got back home to their small two-storeyed villa, Lamise, their mother, took a long and sceptical look at her youngest daughter. She had Hala twirl around, so she could inspect the full results of the makeover. Much as Hala was the apple of her eye, her youngest child, the girl did, still, take too many liberties!

She was glad that all her children had been educated; and especially Saeed, her only boy and the man of the family now; Hala, her youngest, too, who was much like her brother in so many ways. But traditions and conventions were there for a good reason. She would let Hala pursue her Masters here in Dubai, and then, she thought, pleased at the charm of her own liberality, and then, it would be time to be married.

'You're lucky that Maryam, who married so late, has made such a success of her life. It has made me a more open-minded mother. If you marry at twenty-six, say, or twenty-seven, I won't have failed.'

They had one maid in the house, which was as much as they could afford. Saeed promised, daily, that he'd soon be making exponentially more money. His name as a commentator on current affairs was growing, and soon, he kept saying, he would be in a position to 'cash in'. But was it advisable to let him write the way he wrote? Apart from the fact that she hardly understood a word of it and was convinced that none of his readers did either, he really shouldn't question so much, especially not the norms and the mores of this, their beloved homeland. He insisted that his critical work was not there to undermine the phenomenon that was Dubai; if at times he played devil's advocate, well, that was a needed ploy to allow for the possibility of the beatification of a place. She didn't know what 'beatification' meant. He'd explained, teasing her with tales of Catholic ultramontane practice. Yes, he had always been curious as a boy, too curious. He took that, as did Hala, from their father, Abdulaziz. It was only Maryam, her eldest, who took after her. In any case, Saeed was nearly forty now, and he, too, needed to marry, start a family, carry on the family name. By God! How she missed her husband's presence! He was the kind of man who was able, instinctually, to know the right thing to do in every situation. Heart disease and diabetes had been the end of him. Yes, it was time Saeed got married; he had dithered and frittered too long. Soon, no doubt, he would begin to lose his hair!

But when in converse with his mother, or with himself, Saeed was sceptical of a marriage of convenience, which was what might have been expected of him. On the other hand, that didn't mean he was a hopeless romantic. In fact, he was quite conflicted in this area. It was a tart topic of conversational conflict between himself and Hala, who of course bought and ate up the romantic line wholeheartedly.

He'd read the romantics, and indeed believed that they, with their infamous ethos, had done the modern world a good deal of damage. For example, Dubai was often dubbed to be a 'superficial' place. But such pat judgments, automatisms almost, proved obtuse. It was since romanticism that people had got into their heads that superficies were pejorative; it was the influence of the romantics that had led people to forget the integrity of appearances, hunting as they always were for some elusive, supposedly authentic 'depth.' No, to reach the true essence of a thing, one had to go via appearance. The image of Farida, striking, bold, attractive, fluttered through his mind.

He thought of a short story he'd read not too long ago. In it, the author had thematised his take on female psychology. It was a quite deftly executed and brilliant little fiction! The author had one of his characters opine, after some Lacanian insight no doubt, that contingency, flukes and chance were the source of female fascination. The term 'sexy' for the female, perhaps unlike the male, had very little to do with the physical act. No. The female being by her nature a storying creature, who ever totted up each atom of experience from beginning to end, Alpha to Omega, was riveted by mystery, oddness. The chance to render that mystery revelatory, odd turned even – that was what most enticed the female imaginary. A man, who triggers a story in the woman, well, he's got a better chance of attraction. If she, whomever she may be, can't quite pin down the man in question, is forced to construct via her imagination a theory, a story, to make sense of his mystery – well! That guy is in luck!

He recouped his previous line of thought: God! He was a rambler, even to himself! But that was part and parcel of a deep-bedded love for the more contemplative life. There it was again, though: 'love.'

So: love, yes, love, even at its most soulful, entered through the eyes. Only then might it bolster, be bolstered by the I. And Dubai was a feast for the eyes, which, *post festum* – a Latin tag he'd learnt from its use in Marx – became or could become a feast for the soul. For all his liberal and progressive views and for all his westernised experiences, he believed deeply in the ongoing project, virtuoso, sublime, that had made Dubai and the Emirates his homeland for the second time.

*

Later that day, while waiting in a long line of cars at a petrol station to fill up his black sedan, he checked his email, once, twice, three times, to see if his old friend and colleague had replied. He really was eager to see her, to discuss his new, burgeoning projects and ideas. And besides that, it was a good opportunity to re-establish contact after such a shamefully fallow period in their friendship. When just a few days earlier, it had occurred to him to get in contact and pick her mind, he'd realised, with novel force, how much he'd missed their chats. She'd been one of his first friends at the paper where they'd both worked. Rachel (now McGinn) was a rare gem in the media world of mud and sludge. But still, there was no reply.

At this point Saeed's attention was pricked by a small scuffle and ruckus two cars in front. The car being fuelled had finished and, it seemed, paid. But it hadn't moved. It was a pristine and sparkling black Mercedes with tinted windows and bright chrome wheel-spokes. Someone ridiculously rich no doubt, who felt entitled to stop there as long as they (or he – it felt like a he) pleased.

The driver of the next car in line, draped all in black and wearing the hijab, had spent the last minute or so honking loudly, but now got out of her seat to approach the driver stuck in front. Saeed watched the woman, caught between amusement and admiration, as she knocked on the driver's seat's window of the Mercedes. He himself would never have had the gumption! The window dropped slowly and the woman began to give the Mercedes driver a piece of her adamant mind. She was wagging an index finger at the driver, no doubt, Saeed imagined, telling him that she and they didn't have all day!

After the half-minute scolding, the Mercedes began to trundle off, and Saeed was shocked to recognise the woman as Farida. She hadn't been wearing the hijab earlier that morning. But then, yes, it was a women-only salon. He'd forgotten then. And he'd forgotten it again. He was intrigued by the coincidence of coming across her for the second time that day. He couldn't quite make out where his appraisal of her quite came out. Was she just a strong-willed woman? Or was she obnoxious? Thinking how attractive she was – yes, admittedly, *very* attractive – he decided that no, she wasn't obnoxious.

He figured it to himself as follows: she had probably had a hard time of it all her life. She had probably faced more 'reality' than he, even if not necessarily moneyed so to speak, had ever faced himself. The cruel nature of the world for a woman like her – a Muslim ostensibly, a Moroccan immigrant, too – had led her to take the bull by the horns. He knew that for all his facility with words and liberating ideas, he was deeply attached to his routine and the comforts of the predictable. He didn't consider himself a traditionalist, not by any means. But faced by this new striking reality, observing her strangely alluring independence of spirit, he couldn't help but recognise in himself all the hallmarks of a conservative temperament.

The slow, pricking realisation irritated him somewhat. He'd decided. He got out of his car, while Farida was still simmering down, staring with venom at the disappearing Mercedes. He walked past the intervening vehicle and greeted her with a warm and beaming smile. Farida gasped, then rallied herself. Glaring at him with a mixture of annoyance and curiosity, it looked like she was on the verge of saying something to this impertinent man who obviously thought very highly of himself. But she said nothing, though her rouged lips parted slightly.

Saeed continued to smile. Then he said:

'I didn't recognise you.'

'Why should you?' she replied.

'The hijab, I mean.' He'd disarmaments speaking through his eyes. Her mind began to canter; her heartbeats began to think.

'Oh,' she said.

The car behind began honking its horn. The couple, who weren't a couple, were holding up the line.

'Yes,' he now said. 'I'm sorry, by the way, about this morning. I can be so absent-minded.'

'Oh,' she said, 'oh…' She looked at him again, and in the round this time. His almond-coloured eyes, shaped like a gazelle's, were streaked by thyme-green striations. They'd a gentle melancholy to them. She felt strangely uncertain of herself all of a sudden. The car behind was still honking. She peered at him with ungainly intent, but it didn't make him feel awkward. He just looked back, smiling. They were sharing their silence like telepaths beneath the drum of the afternoon sun. The car behind honked once again.

Feeling like he knew something of her character already, Saeed expected her to shout back at the honking, waiting car. But she didn't. She just smiled weakly and Saeed pointed a faint finger at the waiting line. It was a finger both purposive and hesitant at the same time.

'I have to go.' She walked slowly moving tenderly as she sat back in the driving seat, as though suddenly less certain of her own body's movements; as if she were learning again to allow her brain to send signals down her nervous system to the moving limbs.

When she drove off, Saeed stared after her, still standing in the glaring, pounding heat, his mind a melee. Unhorsed, he now thought to himself. He loved the odd medieval metaphor. Unhorsed. And without a sword. And (without a sword) probably due to be slain.

V

After calling him on the new mobile number he'd sent her with his email, Rachel met up that evening with Saeed at the smallish bohemian café he had suggested. The place had both an indoor area and an outdoor terrace. The tables were small and round and the chairs looked delicate and quaint, their shapes like upturned black question marks. It was past *Iftar*, the time of the evening repast after the day's fast, so Saeed was delighting in his cigarette, sipping on a diet Pepsi; Rachel, dressed in a white jumpsuit, was busy perusing the menu. It was her first time at the place. She'd passed it many times, situated as it was on the second floor of a hotel she and Oliver knew well, because Oliver had once organised a small conference in its ballroom, gathering potential investors for a project that was pending at the time. But she'd always passed it by, because the sign on the front read 'Sports Bar'. She'd expected and assumed the place would be filled with shoals of pug-faced compatriots, riotously egging on this or that team on the big screens that no doubt pocked the walls like pedestals, upon which the latest sporting victory or defeat could be lauded or denigrated. But when she entered she found it, as Saeed had forewarned, a quaint and elegant place, with the airs and graces of a bohemian haunt in Soho or Notting Hill. Rachel had introduced Saeed to Notting Hill, years and years back. He'd even dated a Welsh woman who'd lived there. That had been quite the adventure; Rachel, quite naturally, providing the caring ear for her inexperienced Arab friend and colleague.

Imogen-Mary had been Saeed's first real girlfriend. Although he'd been gently set up with a few Emirati girls, mainly the daughters of his mother's friends, by his late twenties Saeed was still relatively inexperienced. He'd been sitting in a Jamaican bar near Portobello Road, tapping his fingers to the groovy music. He wasn't drinking; he didn't drink. And not because of any religious scruple – he just never liked the stuff. A slim woman with cream-white skin, also in her late twenties, was eyeing him from her side of the bar. Saeed pretended not to notice, while still enjoying the lively, upbeat music. She left the bar momentarily, heading for the washroom. Saeed looked furtively round, not finding her seated there anymore. He continued to sip his soda, looking through his aviators at the bottles of alcoholic beverages lined like phalanxes on the shelves behind the bar. Then, shocking him out of his bored perusal, like a jack-in-the-box, the vision of this fair-skinned, blond woman now accosted him as she came over and sat by his side. Her thin body balanced on the bar stool like a spinning top. She had small russet freckles around her nose, and sea-green eyes. She said:

'I've never seen you here before. Who are you?'

She said it forcefully, but not to alienate in any way. It just seemed that she was a forthright, plain-talking kind of girl.

Saeed introduced himself, helplessly gallant.

'My name is Saeed. It is my pleasure to meet you.'

And Imogen-Mary was hooked, partly because *Lawrence of Arabia* was one of her favourite films, and partly because Omar Sharif was one of her favourite actors. She, herself, was a film buff. And though she happened to work at the time as a sales assistant in the Notting Hill branch of Ralph Lauren she aspired to study film one day – in New York, preferably – and hoped to become a world-renowned director.

Saeed spoke in turn of his own recently completed graduate studies and his new role as a journalist. And the conversation, for all the music thumping in the background, had rattled on and on. When they'd left the bar, they'd walked what seemed like the whole of the Kensington area that night, as he'd chatted with this fascinating young Welsh woman before escorting her home.

They'd dated for a few months. But then things, as they usually do, had gone sour. Imogen-Mary had simply been too frightening for the green and tender heart of the young Emirati. And being relatively inexperienced, Saeed had asked Rachel for advice on how to end the relationship. A very sensitive man, he was petrified at the thought of hurting another being, let alone a young woman. Rachel had chuckled, saying:

'Welcome, Saeed, to the adult world!'

She'd given him the best advice she'd been able to muster, informed by who she knew he was, and by what he'd told her of his girlfriend. A few days later, seated at a café on the Kensington High Street, a populated place, as Rachel had advised, to pre-empt the woman at this break-up scene from making a scene, Saeed had said, winding up:

'I wanted to ask.'

Imogen-Mary had small incipient tears in her light emerald eyes. Her pupils were slightly dilated.

'Is there anything you want to know? I mean, any questions you want answered?'

This was a bold and brilliant stroke. Imogen-Mary looked at Saeed, marvelling. How ever did he understand women so well?!

She answered him in the negative. She, too, could be gallant and dignified.

A couple of girls seated on their right, chatting over coffee, looked round at Saeed, hungrily.

Overhearing the manner in which he'd broken up with his girlfriend, they, too, were flabbergasted! And Saeed thanked his lucky stars he'd a friend like Rachel.

Having ordered their meals now, Rachel and Saeed's discussion began in earnest. Saeed asked after her husband and her child, and Rachel glowingly related what she could. Olivia was getting so big! And Oliver was a workaholic with a golden heart. Most days he worked from morning until late at night, moving between offices and meetings, sometimes visiting engineers and architects on various sites. In turn, Rachel asked the questions she wanted to, trying to see what had happened to this loveable man since last they'd met. Saeed said:

'I miss London, the old days. But...'

'But what?' Rachel egged him on.

'What I was going to say was, but: I'm no spring-chicken anymore. I can do my work from anywhere. And to be honest, it's so good to be back in this spilling, excessive princedom. I suppose I'm becoming a tad conservative in my old age.'

'Rubbish,' Rachel replied, laughing him off. 'What are you now? Thirty-five? Thirty-six?'

'Thirty-eight this past May,' he said, sighing wistfully.

'So, what? What are you saying? That you're ready to settle down with a nice Emirati girl? Gosh, you have changed! Your mum will be over the moon! And why not? Maybe it's for the best?'

'Not quite that, Rachel; not yet, at least. But I've reached a point in my life where I want to stop questioning everything and gauging it against some ideal forged in the kiln of a puritanical mind. I need to start making a go of life. You know,' he continued, 'I understand now why as people get older they become less puritanical or idealistic. It's actually simple, and obvious. We're more invested in the world; more compromised, thus. Whether it's a property, a child, a reputation or what have you, by the time you get to our age, well, maybe we are just too much a part of the world to be able to judge it sweepingly from holy heights. Speaking of that...'

'Yes,' Rachel said. 'I read the article you sent me. It's intriguing, though perhaps a touch too highbrow for your readers.'

'Stuff and nonsense,' Saeed said teasingly. 'It's lucid, I think. At least, I hope it is. I tried to explain myself well. I thought I had. So, I haven't?'

'No, it's not that; it's just as you said it's a bit of a mishmash generically. Too colloquial and anecdotal for some thoroughbred scholarly journal, and too ponderously deep for your average op-ed. You know what I'm saying. Imagine if our old editors in London had a gander at a piece like that! There'd be so many changes, you'd have red ink bleeding all over the page!'

'Yes, that's quite true of course.' Saeed composed himself, taking a tug of his cigarette. 'But I'm at an age now, and a stage in my career, where I don't want to have to compromise whatever comes naturally to my intellectual instincts. I mean, that's how one becomes great. By carving out a niche, where the way your particular mind works becomes, hate the term as I do, the equivalent of a kind of brand. Recognition.'

Rachel smiled and winced.

'No, I don't mean vainglory. I mean being recognised as the thinking mind that just does its business this way rather than that.'

They tussled over the ins and outs of it for a while longer. The waiter serving them happened to overhear Saeed say that journalism, the real hale stuff, was not so much dead in Dubai as stillborn, all being overly done at the service of advertising companies. Edouard paused, having lain out their coffees, and remained stood by their table looking at them, without uttering a word. Saeed made a face as if to say, both to Rachel and the hovering waiter, 'Well, this is awkward, isn't it?'

Edouard had been dwelling on his brother's travails for some time – he'd always worried about and for Patrick; and hearing two apparently seasoned journalists talking about media in Dubai, well, it was an opportunity perhaps; a sign of sorts.

Edouard had seen the man before. He was a regular. But he hadn't known that he was a journalist. Apologising now for his staring, stilled there like an obsidian statue, Edouard said:

'Excuse me, sir. But I couldn't help but overhear. You work in media?'

Saeed nodded, generously.

In the space of a minute, with real aplomb, Edouard summarised his brother's situation, and asked for any advice from these two, these eminent, distinguished journalists. Rachel giggled at the man's obsequiousness. She now intervened to say:

'He is in the right place. Dubai is a media-hub. Let him persist, that's all. I'm sure he'll get a break, if he's as smart and resourceful as he seems from what you say.'

Tongue-tied once more, Edouard didn't know how far he might push this situation. But before he could say anything further, seeing him dithering, Saeed whipped out his card and handed it to Edouard, telling him that Patrick should feel free to contact him, or perhaps send him a sample of his work.

As Edouard walked away towards the kitchen, he thanked fortune and all the shapes of the constellations that he'd opted for the evening shift that day.

The two journalists recommenced their conversation. The interruption had served as a segue to a different area of interest.

Rachel asked about Saeed's love-life. She had the prerogative, of course, having been his shoulder to cry on during their London days. Saeed, though, perhaps one of the most balanced, astute men she had known back then, had been strangely inexperienced with women, apart from that Welsh girl and one or two others. Perhaps he'd made up for lost time since coming back to Dubai? But that was unlikely, for obvious reasons. Handsome in a dopey kind of way, intelligent as a razor, but above all else sexy with the sexiness that came with a combined sense of mystery and open-breasted innocence, he should by rights have had a score of relationships by now. Saeed demurred, but blushed slightly.

'Ah! Haha! So: there is someone!' Rachel alighted like a hawk.

He mumbled something self-deprecating and, paying the bill, stood up and helped Rachel out of her chair with a kind of old-world chivalry that quite suited him, with his thick shock of black hair and his bushy eyebrows, dressed in a pristine white *kandura*, the traditional robe of the Emirati male. She asked him if this get-up was permanent. No, he said that of course he also wore 'western' clothing; he wasn't as changed from the London days as all that. And yet, it was actually strangely relieving to see him again, after all this time, wearing the traditional Emirati garb. And she said so.

'Maybe I'm searching for my roots now, with more gusto.' As they ambled slowly out of the place, arm-in-arm in a chummy way which made people look round, Saeed was thinking of someone in particular, who'd begun to put down roots in his heart with as much force, it seemed, as his beloved homeland.

*

In another part of the city, Oliver was having dinner with a sometime business partner. Bassam was a Lebanese financier who'd invested in one of Oliver's projects a couple of years back, and since then, they'd become friends. And this evening, his wife busy with her own friend, he'd decided to match like with like and meet with this slightly younger, but far wealthier, business friend. Both men had been close to ruined by the financial fiasco of 2008. But now soaked in the syrup of renewed success, both men had little compunction reminiscing about the hard times. Bassam said:

'You know, I was even in the red, back in 2008. You won't believe it perhaps, but I was. I didn't even tell my wife. I just put my head to the grindstone, knuckled down, and, thank God, was able to ride through the storm. Things are better now. Much. Looking up, even, wouldn't you say?'

Oliver nodded his head, while munching a mouthful of seafood linguine.

'God this is good!'

Bassam smiled.

'*Suhh-teyn.*'

'*Ala-Elbak.*'

'So: you've picked up some of the lingo, then?'

'Yup. You know, just the kitchen-variety Arabic sayings. It's good for business.'

'Yes, of course.'

Both men were dressed in expensive-looking suits. Bassam's deep burgundy tie was shaped in a power-knot, thick and bold, while Oliver, the chubbier of the two men, had his tie loose from the collar, screwy and misshapen.

'My wife was saying just the other day that it's a shame we don't take our children on play-dates. Jad, my youngest, is about the age of your Olivia, you know.'

Oliver, caught again mid-munch, nodded his head, stooped over his plate as he was.

'Yes, sure. I'll tell Rachel to give May a ring. By the way...'

'Yes?'

'A little birdy told me that you're moving up the echelons – that you've been promoted. So? Head now of the whole of Middle Eastern operation?'

Bassam deprecated, as was his wont.

'It's only a small firm.'

'Small? Your hedge-fund, if I'm not mistaken, manages close to a billion, doesn't it?'

'Something like that.'

'And then there's this.' Oliver straightened up in his seat now, having finished his meal. Bassam had only eaten an appetiser.

'There's what?'

Oliver pulled a magazine out of the small black satchel to the side of his seat. On the front cover of *the* business magazine of the Emirates was a picture of Bassam, stood posing for the camera in a slightly bashful way. The cover's glossy caption spoke in a short punchy phrase of the new up-and-coming generation of business leaders.

'Oh, that.'

'Yes, that. Bloody hell, mate, that's a coup!'

Bassam deprecated, again. That was his nature, Oliver knew well.

About a year after they'd worked together for the first time, Oliver had had a patent and arrowing insight into the nobility of his friend. He'd mentioned to Bassam at that time, casually, that he'd developed a property that simply wouldn't sell. Three days later, a very prominent Emirati had contacted Oliver on his mobile, though Oliver had never met or had dealings with the man, and within twenty-four hours had bought up the property. Oliver had been flummoxed, though delighted, and had only found out a week further on that it was Bassam who'd arranged the contact and the meet. After this, Oliver was determined to give Bassam his cut, a middleman fee that was perfectly appropriate – no, check that, it was non-negotiable! The next time he'd seen Bassam, as they were heading off for dinner at a close-by restaurant, Oliver had handed over a cheque for three hundred thousand dollars. Bassam, though, had refused, placing his right palm over his heart, tenderly, whispering a dignified disclaimer. And though Oliver had insisted he take the finder's fee, had insisted all through dinner and in the days beyond, he'd not been able to shift the cheque. Bassam was the epitome of chivalry, gallantry, quixotry; Oliver admired the man, immensely. And it redoubled his faith in the business world of the Middle East; it wasn't just that it had provided him with opportunities to make the kind of fortune not available elsewhere. It was due to the golden, antique mores of knights errant like Bassam. He'd had a soft spot for the Lebanese ever since.

As both men were drinking that evening, and both resided close to each other in the financial district of Dubai, they shared a taxi home. For the whole cab ride, the two men entertained each other with talk of future projects they might collaborate on. There was a plot of land, Oliver said, that was just begging to be developed! Bassam averred that perhaps now was not the time, there being a glut in the property market. But Oliver pooh-poohed that.

The Indian taxi-driver was mildly amused by the conversation in the back of his cab. The Englishman was evidently drunk, but that was the way of the English. The other man, he looked Lebanese, seemed in complete control of his senses.

Vinod loved the Lebanese. Yes, it was the English who'd given them, Indians, the trappings of modern civilization. And yes, he also entertained the view that, in light of the post-Colonial era, it would have been better for India (and Pakistan, he supposed, which would in any case not have become Pakistan in the first place) had the English taken a slower, more considered time to retreat out of the country. But Churchill was a bugger; yes, he was a bugger. The Lebanese, by turns, he found always to be successful people. He'd heard it said that they were like the Armenians in this. By mundane fate, they were eminently dynamic as a people. They'd been forced to be, challenged by geography and by history to excel. A friend of his had once said of the Lebanese, mild with jest, that once, as Phoenicians, they'd been a nation of merchant-sailors, infamous around the Fertile Crescent and beyond; and that now, the lucky bastards, they were all merchant bankers!

In any case, Bassam's home being the second stop, the Lebanese man supplemented the owed fare with a good twenty-dirham tip. Which only confirmed it – the Lebanese were stars. And Hakim would be jealous. And yes, Vinod made sure to make a mental note to inform his old Pakistani partner of all the dripping *baksheesh* he'd made that night. The Eid was only a day or two away, and it delighted him to think that it was he, the non-Muslim, who was benefitting from the generosity of the customers during this sacral time. Hah!

VI

'It's settled,' Saeed announced, poking his head through the doorway. 'The Eid is the day after tomorrow.' He returned to the innards of the neighbouring room, where his library and his workspace were.

'There is no greater than God!' His mother Lamise clapped her hands in delight.

'And there is no lesser than me.' Hala was in a huff. Yet another conversation with her mother in which the latter persisted, persisted, persisted in forbidding her to take up her place at Queen Mary, London, where she so wished to pursue her MA in literature and gender studies.

'It's the perfect place for it!' Hala said. 'I've seen the course outline and the modules being offered, and it's perfect for what I want to do.'

'What you *think* you want to do.'

'No, what I *want* to do.' Hala looked fiercely at her mother, who merely sighed away the look like it was a firefly. 'And the faculty there; don't get me started on the faculty. I'd never find such experts here in Dubai. In Sharjah, maybe, but...'

'Sharjah?' The idea piqued.

'No, you can forget that, Mother. I'm certainly not going to study in Sharjah!'

'But Sharjah is a kind of "abroad", isn't it?' Lamise was warming to the idea.

'You want me to go hooded, is that it?'

Her mother briefly put on a mask like a wounded seal.

'I take it back,' said Hala. 'Listen, I'm fine with wearing the hijab now and then, when it's expected of me. But you know very well how much more traditionalist Sharjah is than Dubai.'

'Ah.' Her mother pounced. 'I knew it. So, you do want to study in Dubai?' Lamise hadn't realised the implicit circularity in her reasoning. Or, rather, she had, but was hoping that a little bit of finessing sophistry might work.

'Oh!' Hala covered her face with both her hands, as though she were about to start weeping.

Saeed now walked into the living room and saw the tableau vivant, as it were. His mother on his right hand, staring and stilled at his younger sister on his left. He thought to himself that he was not only now standing between them in the room, but that symbolically, too, he was like a bridge between the two extremes of age and youth, tradition and adventure. Lamise now said:

'I just don't understand what it is that is so alluring about London?!' She looked plaintively at her son, as though begging for his timely intervention. But Saeed remained impassive.

'Mother, I've just explained what it is,' Hala said.

'Well,' Saeed intervened, 'let's not let this little scuffle spoil our Eid.' He shot a surreptitious glance at his sister, indicating that now was not the time. His mother failed to notice, and moved towards the doorway at the farther end of the room, talking as she went.

'Perhaps I'm too old to understand the young. But I know what's best for my youngest child. I'm going in for a nap. Wake me if Maryam and Walid come over later. I'm tired, bone-tired. I feel like I've an army of *djinns* besieging my head.' She walked out of the room, rubbing her temples rhythmically, leaving the two of them standing there, as if in cahoots.

Saeed paused for a while, wandering slowly, errantly round the room, now and then picking up an ornament or two from some of the shelves that decked the walls of that room, inspecting them with a lightsome, querulous air, and then placing them back. It seemed as if his movements were dramatising his approach to a tricky subject. After a minute or so, he came close to his sister and said:

'Look. Don't worry. I have it on the best authority that you will be permitted to go to London in autumn.'

'Whose authority? Whose, Saeed, whose?'

'Well, my own of course. Am I the man of this family, or am I not? Just give me some time. She's slowly warming to the idea, I can tell.'

'She is not!'

'Take it from me, your brother who loves you, who's spent well over a decade getting to know and love (and hate, at times, admittedly) the wily ways of a widow and matriarch. Trust me. I think, I'm quite confident I'll be able to wangle it. Just lie low for the meantime, would you? Let her think she's had her way. We'll move in for the kill when the time is right. And two days before Eid certainly is not the right time!'

Hala wiped away her furtive tears, and smiled wetly up at her brother.

'But...' Saeed said.

'Yes?'

Saeed smiled, coyly.

'But it's going to cost you.'

'What do you mean?'

'I'll be wanting a favour in return.'

'Anything, Saeed. But what could it be?'

Saeed dithered, and a small, creeping inkling crept up Hala's spine. It had occurred to her, very briefly the day before. Something did seem to have sparked between him and Farida. But she'd dismissed the idea. Now, however, she leapt at the thought, both figuratively and literally.

'Ah! I see.'

'Perhaps you do?'

'It wouldn't be that my cerebral older brother, my intellectual, my serious-minded older brother, has a crush on someone, would it?'

'It's more than a crush.'

'Good. So, it's more than a crush. Good.'

'At my age, one doesn't get crushes. The weight on the heart is of a different timbre.'

He was intrigued. He was compelled. To him, Farida was like an ingenious argument delivered by the doyen of philosophers, convincing his heart with Ciceronian eloquence. He found her looks deeply enticing. He found the strength he'd sensed in her even more so. True, he'd only spoken to her twice. True, it might all be a ruse, played upon him by his loneliness. But something had clicked. It was like he was a schoolboy again, studying his mathematics or his physics, not understanding the equations, but then suddenly, it all clicked into place, and the world of numbers opened up like a grand boulevard for the mind! Like a cog in the machine of his heart.

'So, you want her number, is that it?'

'Well, I know you're friendly with all the women at that salon, and Eid's coming up, and I thought, well, it might be romantic in a kind of absurd way...'

Hala clapped her hands together, a gesture that was identical to the one performed by her mother a short time earlier. She jumped up and down a couple of times, delighted. Saeed, alarmed, tried to calm her excitement.

'I see,' said Hala. 'You don't want Mother to know, is that it?'

'Not yet. No, not yet.'

Arm-in-arm, sister and brother walked out of the house into the small orchard of the garden, where Saeed proceeded to question Hala about this Moroccan woman.

*

It was deep into night-time now, and all in the household had retired. Maryam and Walid had visited earlier that evening, but then had left. Hala had read in her room well into the night but was now sound asleep. Lamise, too, had just fallen into slumber, having watched some Turkish melodrama on her tablet, the one concession she paid to the digital age in which they lived.

Saeed could not understand why women of a certain advanced age – he'd seen it many times – found these damned contrived soap operas so enjoyable. When asked once, his mother had answered that it forced her to empathise and that the purging emotions she felt when spellbound by such shows actually relaxed her. It had reminded him of his London days. He'd once quipped to a male friend that the football every weekend was the equivalent of Attic tragic drama; that Aristotle's theory in his small treatise on poetics applied perfectly; that if the predominantly working-class football fans didn't have this spectacle each weekend where they could vent all the burdens and frustrations of what was and might always be an unjust world, well, there would have probably been more than one revolution there.

Presently, he was staring at the mobile number his sister had written out for him in her large and round spidery hand. He certainly wasn't going to call Farida. Hala had said that a text would be fine. She'd said that, knowing Farida as well as she did, she wouldn't think it too forward or too awkward or anything like that. 'She's a warrior, a woman of sense and plain talking. You'll see.'

He'd learnt quite a bit about the woman from his sister earlier that day, as the two of them had strolled round and round their orchard, serenading the sunset with the lowered tones of their gentle conversation. And whether he was deluding himself or not, he prided himself on his sixth sense. He felt, in short, that the rest he needed or wanted to know he could figure out by himself. Still staring at the mobile number penned in blue ink, he continued to consider.

'Longing for the nearness that was far.' It was a phrase he'd read in the work of some German metaphysician. Perhaps it meant very little. Perhaps it was a profound formulation. Then he thought of a motif in Ovid; yes, in Ovid, if he wasn't mistaken. It was the idea that lovers should search for and devote their adoration not to the perfections of their beloved, but to the blemishes. Which made sense. If one could love the worst, then it went without saying that the good, the better and the best would be a doddle. He didn't give a damn that Farida was a divorcée, but he knew his mother would. But then, he didn't really care much about that, either. Not now, at least, at this stage in his life. He loved his mother deeply and felt increasingly tender about her as they both grew older. But a man who wanted to call himself one had to ultimately face a moment of decision, if he wasn't to let life, in all its vast richness, pass him by. Which reminded him of Henry James, and how in one of his more well-known stories and in one of his late and quite ingenious novels, this was his central theme. Waiting for the right moment obsessively, on primed tenterhooks, could end up meaning, quite deftly, that it had passed you by like a slow and loping bullet in the meantime. No. He was certain that in the weave of a life that hoped and aimed to be a flourishing one, you had to pay dues to chance, to coincidence, to the flukes and contingencies you never saw coming, winging their way into your horizon from a different atmosphere, a different galaxy, a different universe, even. Life was full of surprises. That was a dead phrase, a cliché. But clichés were clichés for a reason.

Still, he glared at the number on the paper in front of him. His eyes glazed over. He felt, oddly, like his whole life was being held in summary – summarily, too – in the hand of God. He pressed his lips together emphatically, gently thumped a clenched fist onto the wood of his desk. He picked up his mobile and, entering the number, wrote the following text:

Hello Ms Farida. This is Saeed, Hala's brother. We met only yesterday, twice. Forgive me if this is forward. I wanted to ask you, if I might, if you were doing anything on the evening of the Eid. I know it's a funny thing to ask. But I was hoping we might meet for a chat over a coffee. What say you? With warmest regards, Saeed.

There was nothing beautiful or poetic about the message, and that's how he wanted it. That's how, he felt, she might want it. He couldn't put his finger on why he was so sure, after speaking to her briefly only twice, that he knew her so well. It was like a strangely assured instinct; like the rote movement of a wholly new limb. A new limb, though, at thirty-eight years of age?!

Wasn't it a bit late in the day to harbour such puppy-like love? But was it even love? How could it be? He'd spoken to her only twice.

'We met only yesterday, twice.'

'We only met yesterday, twice.'

Alternating depth-grammar held and pitted the two formulations against each other, like two sparring pugilists. One was a rock, perhaps, the other a hard place.

He felt all of a sudden that his world – the world he'd made for himself, living in the arcane bower of his own erudite mind – had been opened up by a fault-line. The tectonic plates of his being were shifting. Eruptions of white-hot, heart-coloured lava threatened to spill their serpentine way into the close and cosseted township he'd made of a life of practised solitude. But maybe what he called solitude was only loneliness. There was a nice distinction to be made here. Solitude was being alone, with oneself, and with God. Loneliness, well, it had no echo chamber. Was that the difference between a monologue and a soliloquy? Thoughts such as these continued to rush through his mind. Maybe he was going crazy? Maybe he was.

VII

Eid was on the following day, so the grocery store was far busier and more bustling than usual. All of Dubai, moneyed or mendicant, was stocking up for the festivity. Ricardo had had more bagging and delivery work than usual, and it wasn't even eleven o'clock yet! He called out to Patrick now, to help him with the bagging. But Patrick, standing a matter of metres behind him, had failed to hear. He was daydreaming again. Ricardo called to him a second time, but Patrick was rubbing a small paper or piece of card between his fingers, staring down at it glassy-eyed. It was a shame – Patrick shouldn't have been working in the store in the first place. Neither should he, for that matter! But Ricardo had a soft spot for the young Ugandan gentleman, built like a heavyweight boxer, yet still child-like in his continuous daydreaming. So, he desisted and continued to do all the bagging himself, glad to let his friend fantasise the morning away.

Sharing a cigarette outside a couple of hours later, during their ostensible lunch break, which only lasted twenty minutes in any case, Patrick had let on at last what had happened.

'This is my ticket.' Gesturing to the well-clutched card, he then tucked it away and framed a wide, grand silver screen above his brow with both his hands, indicating fame and success. The skin on his hands was soft, despite his pugilist-like build.

'And where are you headed?' Ricardo was quite capable of irony. He pointed at the sky above their heads, as though to gently mock the grand stage of success and fame that his friend had just invoked.

'To CNN. With, of course, a few pitstops on the way.'

'So, the guy gave you his card, just like that, for the blue of your eyes; or for the blue of your brother's?'

'He did. And no, not for nothing. My eyes are dark brown anyway. My brother's eyes are too.'

Ricardo chuckled.

'No, it wasn't for nothing. Edouard can be quite convincing. I don't like to say it, because he's resigned himself to a life of service and never shows any ambition, but my brother is even smarter than me.'

'What makes you so smart, then?'

'I read.'

'*I* read.'

'Ah,' Patrick continued, entering into his stride, 'but it's what you do with the information. It's the way you store it, arrange it, rearrange it. It's the way you can toy with it.'

Ricardo, delighted, alighted:

'I'm buying my little one his toy dinosaur this evening. God! He's going to jump up and down so much when I give it to him!'

'I thought it was for his birthday?'

'His birthday falls on the Eid this year. Who'd have thought it? Perhaps that is the wily way of God the Father, God the Son and God the Holy Spirit?'

Patrick grinned wryly, his pearly teeth stark against his dark acidic skin. But he wasn't to be sidetracked.

Having been gifted by fate, he was planning to try his luck and send his manuscript to Saeed. It was a shame he'd not been able to afford a laptop as yet, and that he'd had to write the whole thing by hand. Or maybe it wasn't? Maybe it was more oaken, in a writerly manner, to have written his book in the old way.

He decided on his plan. He would write to Saeed, politely, deferentially, and ask him to meet, perhaps, so that he could hand him the manuscript, which was only in hard copy. He pictured their conversation in anticipation. He would deliver a monologue on the reasons why he'd written the book with a black and then a blue pen. He would talk about the banes of the digital era, and how it dispersed the rights of authorship, authority. But not too much, perhaps?

He didn't want to seem a slowcoach, woefully behind the times.

'I've written a book, you see.'

Ricardo disbelieved. Patrick expostulated. At last convinced that it wasn't a hairbrained fantasy, the Filipino asked what it was about, stubbing out his cigarette. And Patrick told him of it in a glorious précis.

'And so, am I in it?'

'Of course not. I wrote it before I knew you that well.'

'Now that's a shame! My Shirley will be displeased!' Ricardo excelled, in fact, at irony.

But his chummy glibness did nothing to dampen Patrick's spirits. The Ugandan now walked back into the shop, taking up his sturdy position standing near the door, in his black trousers and white shirt with the small red triangular logo over his heart, and twiddled his thumbs as he stood there, thinking briefly of the forthcoming Eid and what it might bring to all of them, all so different, all so alike, but all God's children.

*

'It is my little one's birthday tomorrow,' Shirley was saying over a cigarette.

The salon was extra busy, for obvious reasons.

'Oh! I didn't know that!' Farida was trying to concentrate. She hadn't told Shirley of the text message she'd received late the night before, nor of her response. They were both standing just outside the backdoor of the salon, by the ashtray. On these brief breaks, taken in this deserted lot, they couldn't be seen by anyone, so because it was only for a few minutes, Farida hadn't replaced her hijab.

'I like your hair like this, you know,' said Shirley. For the first time in a long while, Farida no longer sported a bird's nest. Instead, her long and wavy hair serenaded her face like a flattering mane. She looked palpably different, Shirley was thinking – more different than a mere change of hairstyle might render. Something had changed. If she hadn't known better, the bloom on Farida would have indicated new pregnancy. But she did know better.

'So, Eid. What will you be doing?' Farida said.

'Ah. Every year we go for a picnic. Ricardo and Adam and I. And this year, because it is my Adam's birthday as well, we will let him play all afternoon. There is a very good play area we know. It has all the rides and games. And on both sides, there are tables and chairs. We can watch over our boy while we sip delicious coffee. Expensive, yes. But it's our small tradition. We spoil ourselves. It's going to be a special Eid, I know it!'

Farida thought so too.

The whole morning she had kept taking furtive looks at their manager there, her fellow Moroccan. Farah was a good fifteen or so years older than Farida, though she'd been in Dubai for roughly the same amount of time. Farah, too, was divorced. And she, too, as far as Farida knew, had not planned on making the same mistake twice. That said, Farida's divorce had been at a very young age, and a long time ago.

But why on earth was she thinking of wedlock, even ruptured wedlock? She berated herself in silence, violently. It was only a text message, and it was only a coffee. She tried to put the thought of Saeed out of her mind, boggling as he was. She tried to busy her mind, but it kept spinning, like wheels within wheels. Maybe it was time to broach the thought? Maybe there was something brewing in the winds of chance; or, better, maybe her Maker had plans for her? She tussled, agonising, storying this way and that, picturing a litany of scenarios. Each one had a slightly different outcome. But in each one Saeed's dopey smile and the light brown seas of his eyes seemed to make her somehow light-hearted and warmed. All this was new territory for her, a blank spot on the map of her weathered life. But how was it to be filled? With a conqueror, or a peacemaker? Her thoughts continued to spin and spin, slowly growing out of control. She'd always thought that the map of her life was all already chartered space. That she knew all those countries, oceans. That there was no, that there would never be any Columbus at hand. The new world and the old world, as she phrased it to herself, the new and the old...

But then, thankfully, there was some work at hand to busy herself with, so she was able, for a while at least, to put her wandering thoughts at bay.

Because after the lunch break – in which she neither ate nor drank, but smoked – as she re-entered the salon, she asked the receptionist who her afternoon appointment was. It was an English lady whose name she didn't recognise. Farida asked the receptionist, but she didn't know the name either. She asked Shirley, but even she didn't know her, and hadn't worked on her. She finally queried of Farah, who said that yes, the client was apparently new. Which was strange. Of course, they'd had new clients joining their clientele all the time, but it didn't make sense that a woman worth her salt would try out a new salon on the day before Eid, when makeovers were delivered in a more urgent and pressing fashion. True, she was an English woman, but that meant nothing really. Look at Shirley; she was Filipino, and saw Eid as a day of sacral celebration just as much as the local Emirati. So, later that afternoon, Farida asked the new client – Mrs Rachel McGinn – to spill the beans, having succeeded in charming her into talking.

'Oh, I know what you're going to say; I said it to myself, over and over, this morning. But it seems the woman who usually does my hair went to the Philippines and never came back. I had an appointment with her booked from over a month ago. The salon only informed me this morning. Poor girl. She'd returned to be married. But maybe, I don't know, maybe she got pregnant and decided not to return?'

Rachel paused here, worried. Did the supposition sound condescending or belittling? That was the last thing she had intended. But Farida smiled graciously, with her eyes as well as her mouth. She had a row of chunky white teeth which pronounced her good health. And she warmed to this English woman.

'Well,' she said, 'it is our good fortune then.'

The three women – English, Moroccan and Philippine, all so different, all so alike – settled into a long and slow conversation for the next two hours or so, wiling away the afternoon with beautifications. When it came time for Mrs Rachel McGinn to appraise the results, she looked at her face and hairdo in the mirror, at different sideways angles, and said:

'You've won me over, Farida. I'll be coming again, of course. Thank you my dear. I couldn't have wished for a more insightful job.'

The adjective didn't jar. Both Farida and Shirley, and Farah for that matter, who herself hadn't been a manager forever – all of them found it easy to countenance the idea of a makeover being 'insightful'. Aesthetics and cosmetics were, after all, the gateway to the soul. You simply couldn't make your way in the world – a world made of surfaces before anything else – otherwise. Which didn't mean that all of them eschewed depth. No – it only meant that they understood, as independent women in a world of blinkered slaves, that love entered the soul, the heart, the bones, the marrow, every cell and corpuscle, via the eyes.

Farida walked Mrs Rachel McGinn to the door of the salon and wished her and hers a very happy Eid.

Her driver took ten minutes to arrive, and the heat was prohibitive. Getting into the large four-by-four, she was flustered, internally and externally. It was still hours before the last *Iftar* of that Ramadan season, and she needed to be dropped off home by five at the latest, to give her chauffeur Tariq time to both take and pick up Olivia from her ballet class, and to be in time to feast with his own family, on this last evening of the holy month.

About five minutes shy of home, their vehicle got caught up in an unholy logjam. Traffic lights in Dubai, especially at an intersection like this, took inordinate times to change colour, giving each of the four sides of said intersection well over a minute to unburden the road of its build-up. A taxi which had cut them up a minute earlier was now standing still on their right side, waiting for the traffic light to turn green.

Hakim had to give over the car to Vinod in under an hour. The exchange point might take up to an hour to get to, given the chock-a-block traffic that was inevitable this evening. And God knew that if he were even ten minutes late to that exchange, the company would fine him up to five hundred dirhams! Hakim cursed, then cursed again. Then he apologised to the Deity who had placed him now in this pickle. It was a kind of penance perhaps. Or maybe some kind of holy test. As he was cogitating thus, he heard shouting to his left. He turned to see Tariq, a fellow Pakistani, yelling curses down at him, so he opened the window, to reply in kind.

'You! You Pakistani bastard! Who taught you to drive?!'

'You're the Pakistani bastard!' Hakim thrilled to a shouting match like this. It relieved him some-what of his angst about the inevitability of the fine he would have to pay for being late to the hand-over of his cab to Vinod.

These moneyed people. The rich! He peered at the back seat of the four-by-four. Some hoity-toity 'Madam' and her wog-like driver. At least he, Hakim, a statesman among cab-drivers, made an honest living rather than being subservient to the coloniser!

The two brown-skinned drivers emptied their lungs at each other for a few moments more. Then, both men stopped and just looked at each other, as though dumbfounded and at a loss. It was almost as if they were about to burst into mutual, full-bellied laughter, compatriots again, united most of all in their hard luck, and having gifted each other the opportunity to vent.

The pale salmon-coloured lips of both men were shivering. They stared at each other in silence still.

Rachel now opened her window and stuck her head out. She apologised to Hakim, on behalf of herself and her driver.

'I'm deeply sorry, sir,' she said again. 'Please, let's stop this fighting.'

Hakim's grimace softened. Tariq's did too. It was the last evening of Ramadan.

VIII

Later that evening Olivia asked her mother what they were doing on the following day. With a child's wondrous logic, she then asked what the 'Eid' in fact was. All her friends at the nursery were talking about 'Eid', and how it was miraculously toy-filled. So, Rachel tried to explain to her what Islam was all about – the Prophet, the Holy Book, the peacefulness and the utter, utter devotion. Olivia now retorted:

'Oh, I know all about Islam, Mummy.'

Olivia regaled her mother with talk about all her 'Muslim' friends, like Nour and Nada and Shireen. But they didn't fast, because fasting was only for the grown-ups.

'Do they have Muslims in England, Mummy? And do they fast, Mummy? In England I mean?'

Rachel did her best to explain that of course there were Muslims in England. There were Muslims everywhere. And, of course they fasted.

'Are we Christians?'

'Well, yes, you and Daddy are.'

'Aren't you, Mummy?'

Rachel wanted to say that she was agnostic – unlike Oliver, who'd grown into his faith with age, though he didn't do much about it. But that might be a touch too difficult for her daughter to understand. For God's sake, even some of the local authorities couldn't quite swallow the idea of an agnostic. And she then realised that her invoking God's sake was a paradox – a bit like how her father had been wont to say decades ago to her own mother, after she would berate him for some staple misdemeanour, 'Ah, yes, my dear. You're quite right. And I apologise. I must remember to be less absent-minded in future.' The memory made her smile. But no, she wasn't going to tell her daughter yet about her beliefs.

When she'd first arrived in Dubai, getting her resident ID card as a dependant of her husband, she'd asked to put 'agnostic' on the requisite space on the form. Oliver had moaned desperately and urged her to not make undue trouble and just put Christian. As it turned out, some functionary who'd possibly heard wrong, and after she'd insisted, had put that she was a gnostic. And it had become a running in-house joke between her and her husband. Whenever he wanted to tease her, he always said, 'Well, perhaps that makes sense for a gnostic, but not for me.' Or, 'Well, perhaps that's what a gnostic might think of doing in that situation?' And so on.

'Yes, Olivia,' she said at last. 'I am a Christian, just like you and Daddy.'

Dubai was an overtly cosmopolitan space. What she'd most liked about the article Saeed had asked her to read – the first of a series he'd planned, as she gathered – was that he'd averred in it that Dubai was a success story precisely because it didn't try to countenance such cosmopolitanism by creating some wishy-washy, overly liberal and ultimately mendacious middle ground. No. One had the local population, who were the only true bona fide citizens, and one had the vaster majority of expats, from all over. The country and the princedom had kept their Islamic identity intact. The expats knew where they stood as guests. And this overt advert to alterity was healthy. As Saeed had said in his article, 'the other', respected precisely as a wholly distinct 'other', meant that the mutual respect and the mutual tolerance was workable, rather than being some kind of melding façade, as she'd experienced via her deep knowledge of the Lebanon.

In fact, nearly all her Lebanese friends – and she had many in Dubai, primarily through Oliver's work – were voluble in their cynicism about their homeland. They all praised Dubai as quite a different kettle of fish. And yet, though they weren't all Muslims, it did remain the case that they were Arabs. She wondered now if that made it easier for them, with their children? To make the right decisions, on a daily basis? She worried, more than Oliver ever did; she over-worried. And her political nous only fuelled that worry. For all the security and stability of Dubai, she thought to herself, adapting Donne, no country and no princedom is an island. And the contemporary world, both in and around the Gulf region, and beyond – that world seemed to be slowly coming apart at the seams. As she walked her four-year-old now to her bedroom, she noticed the fragility of her own steps. They were like a totem for all her worries.

Even if there was now a Ministry for Happiness in Dubai, she was still unsure of her own. Oh, she loved Oliver of course. And she'd lay her life down for her little girl. But still, it was difficult being so far from home, her parents, her siblings, and Oliver's, too. She also missed her job and that sense of purpose it gave her. Catching herself in the act, she mentally slapped herself across the face. You silly cow! Here you are, living in the lap of luxury, and you're bloody-well complaining. You silly, silly cow!

Tucked in, her arms wrapped round her teddy bear now, Olivia whispered:

'Good night, Mummy; we're going to have the best Eid ever.'

'Good night, munchkin; yes, we are.'

*

In a different part of that large and populous metropolis, Hakim was enjoying the last *Iftar* of the Holy month in the company of friends and co-religionists.

He entered the smallish hut and was presently offered mint tea the colour of oak and dark-hued amber; as well as some locally roasted '*hein-nab*', a bean-small, light-green and red fruit like jujube. Served thus, he entered the *majlis* – a long rectangular room one entered barefoot, lined with gathered cushions for floor-level seating along its wood-walled rims. There were framed pictures across all four walls, a space for commemorating Dubai, its history. As expected, of course, there were the photographs of Dubai's leaders, past and present, as well as those of the UAE more generally – along with their royal offspring. On the other walls there were a surprising mix of ornaments. Along with pictures of President Bush and Prince Charles and Cherie Blair, who had evidently visited the area, were framed newspaper clippings also gratifying to the neighbourhood and its denizens. The famed football player Kaka was also seen grinning in a group photo with the lads from the *majlis*, the local community centre. There were also historical photos from the 1950s and before, showing in one of their black-and-white corners the earlier equivalent of Bur Dubai, this suburb of the miracle city. It was incredible to the accustomed eye of what was now contemporary Dubai, as such photographs showed a far more sparsely built area; indeed, half the space framed was empty sandy wastes. And yet, decades of gruelling heritage were intimated.

The space of the *majlis* was also used, even off-season, for family outings and meals, and one was just as likely to see youths twiddling on their smart-phones here, as much as people like Hakim himself, still wedded to tradition. The walls were lined with wooden strips that looked much like bamboo, but Hakim knew that they were actually palm-wood. Hakim knew in his pride, as well, that this was not only because of the local supply, but also because this type of wood served to keep out the heat – a more handcrafted version of modernised AC.

All the men were served *za'atar* tea in small, cello-shaped tea-glasses, hot thyme-infused water, the colour of electric lemons tinged by hints of lightened honey. As they settled down now to the main meal to be shared, they could hear the odd fishing-boat sound across the water outside, the water whose colour turned deep-crocodile beneath the night sky, striated by slanting, wobbling yellow lines, which were the hazy, watery reflections of the streetlamps lining the creek.

As was the custom in this area, they ate fish this evening. The fish was grilled on live coals, which gave it a more smoky, authentic flavour. And after the meal, Hakim went for a lonesome stroll along the side of the creek. He ambled along with his hands clasped behind his back, thinking of his life in the scheme of things.

It was less hot and humid than might have been expected at that time of summer. He thought now of how both his father and grandfather had gone blind due to bouts of chickenpox, which was at the time one of many life-threatening epidemics. He also thought of the locally imbibed and well-known poem or ditty, often hummed by his friends among the locals. It was native to the creek area and was about how disease had anchored here 'like a boat' and had spread, taking the 'finest people' in its wake. He thought of his four sons back home in Pakistan. They were no doubt getting bigger, stronger. He thought of his wife, Jamila.

Yes. He was grateful; grateful for so much.

*

When Ricardo got home that evening, toy dinosaur in tow, his three-year-old son Adam leapt up at him, to grab his present.

'Not till tomorrow, son, it is not your birthday yet.'

Tears threatened. But Shirley walked over from the kitchen, and one stern look from her stayed the boy's incipient outburst. He muffled his protests and hugged his mother round the knees.

'All set for tomorrow?' asked Ricardo.

'All set.'

'So, we go for the picnic in the morning. Then...'

'Yes,' Shirley continued his thought, 'then we go to the Mall. The play area there is the perfect place for Adam.'

Ricardo exhaled. It was going to be expensive. But worth it of course, for the double-barrelled occasion. They would picnic nearby, in Bur Dubai. At least that would be free of charge. Yes, he most definitely looked forward to carving out their own niche on the wide green lawns near the metro station, the ones surrounded by borders of small, short fuchsias. He looked forward to unravelling the spread he knew his wife had prepared with telling, meticulous care. He looked forward to giving his son his dinosaur toy and seeing him play with it. He looked forward to a holiday from bagging and delivering goods. He looked forward to the Eid.

Adam talked garrulously on different hopping subjects as he was being tucked away in bed. He often did this, when about to go to sleep. He was considering what for him was a very weighty decision – what to call his toy dinosaur. He liked the name Benedict, primarily because it was, he knew, his uncle's name and his grandfather's, both being still in the Philippines. So, the Tyrannosaurus Rex was duly dubbed Benedict in advance of the special day. And when Shirley reported this to her husband, who was squatting down, fiddling with the stereo in the living space of their small apartment, he felt a sudden touch of tenderness.

The night sky outside the window was a deep, ominous periwinkle. The streets below were far quieter than usual. Shirley wrapped her arms around her husband's shoulders and neck and kissed him.

ABBA could be heard strumming their chansons into the night, the volume low, but still enchanting.

They danced; slow and close and sure.

IX

Lamise was the first to awake that day, God be praised. Ablutions made, she walked with an even, steady gait into the kitchen, to find Salima, their Indonesian maid, preparing breakfast. It wasn't an overly large kitchen, not as spacious as she may have wished for, but today of all days it was forbidden to make complaints.

It was late morning. Before either Saeed or Hala emerged from their slumbers, her grandson Walid entered the kitchen from the backdoor of the house, having given a brief, peremptory knock. He went over to his grandmother and kissed her on the cheeks. When asked, he said that his parents were still asleep, but he had wanted so much to wish his beloved granny the staple formulaic wish on the Eid, which meant that the recipient's forthcoming year might be filled with an equal bundle of goodness and happiness and so on.

It didn't occur to Lamise that her grandson might have ulterior motives. When she presently handed over his Eid gift, a nice, thick sum of dirham notes,

Walid pretended that he was surprised, shocked. This made his grandmother laugh. Such a modest, decent-mannered boy!

Hala walked into the kitchen now, in her light grey nightgown.

'Got your cash, have you!?' She smiled down at her nephew mischievously.

Walid blushed slightly, nodding his head.

'Well, and this is from me, and from your uncle Saeed. He's still sleeping, the lazy bum.'

She handed him a clutch of notes of equal thickness to the one from his grandmother. Walid dared not count all the money he'd received, but fingered the wad in his pocket, praying to the Deity that it was a sufficient sum for the Brazil jersey he so desperately wanted to buy. He was of course dressed in the traditional garb, newly purchased, that his parents and relatives wanted him to wear for this sacred day. It comprised a young boy's *kandura* and a pair of elegant slippers. His hair was gelled back just as he liked it. If it meant money, if it meant the Brazil jersey he could show off to his friends, wearing what was expected of him was an easy duty.

'You look like a prince, my dear, my heart,' said Lamise.

Walid replied that he wore it especially to honour the memory of his grandfather. He'd been told to say this by his mother.

'May you bury me.' It was a staple Arabic phrase, again, though not as native to the Gulf as elsewhere in the Arab region; but Lamise liked to use it often for the joy of it when moved by tenderness, indicating as it did unconditional love. She'd got in the habit of using it, because her Turkish soap operas were dubbed in the Syrian idiom.

When Saeed walked into the kitchen, about half an hour later, all four of them sat down to a very, very late breakfast.

In accordance with tradition, they said the noonday prayers together, listening the while to the soaring, melancholic sound of the *muezzin* in the distance. Then they tucked in.

Lamise ogled her son on this happy day. He looked, as he did most mornings, too scruffy. His thick black hair was gawky and unruly, and he needed to shave. Oh, she knew of course that her son was more concerned with his mental life, less with his external appearance. And yes, that was what made him so special; she was very proud to have a son with such a mind! Even if he often lost her with his talk and with his writings, she was proud, frequently bragging of his intellect and his achievements to her friends. But still, he needed to preen himself more. Why he still refused to use the lotion she'd given him, she couldn't fathom. This morning, as ever, he had light grey bags beneath his eyes, which she knew wasn't due to lack of sleep. No, she had the same genetic predisposition, as did Maryam. Hala, the lucky thing, never had black rings beneath her eyes.

After breakfast Walid returned with his winnings to the small villa next door. Lamise went to her bedroom, to get ready for the ladies' afternoon gathering she was invited to later that day. Hala and Saeed were left alone in the small round salon of the house.

'So?' said Hala.

'So, what?'

'You ready for this evening? Oh, Saeed, she's such a lovely woman!'

'Yes, I'm sure. It's only coffee, you do know that, right?'

'Yes, but I know it's going to work out. I dreamt of both of you, last night.'

'Oh? Please do share?'

'I was walking in the desert. Up and down, over and around, dune after dune. It was midday, and the light was scorching, but it wasn't hot, no, not at all. It was strangely temperate. I was thirsty, though. I kept seeing this oasis, maybe just a mirage, flashing and shimmering in the distance. So I kept on trying to reach it. And then, after traipsing beneath the gruelling sun for what seemed like hours, the oasis had disappeared. But then I looked back, behind me, across the miles of dunes I'd already traversed, I saw the oasis again, this time situated, somehow, in a place I'd already passed. Then I heard a hawk squawk. It had a baby in its beak. It swooped down and laid the baby in the shallow water of the oasis. And suddenly, I didn't feel thirsty anymore.'

'Now that's an elaborate fable!' Saeed exclaimed. 'But where do we come in?'

'Nowhere. You know what dreams are like – I just felt that you were both there at the same time, looking on.'

'Ah, I see.'

'Well, you're the genius,' she said sarcastically. 'What do you think it means?'

'I've no idea,' her brother replied, just as tartly.

'Well, I think it's a good omen.'

Saeed now got to thinking in earnest about his coffee date that evening. He would shave, of course he would. But something held him back from preparing too elaborately for the meeting with Farida. In fact, the way he felt surprised him somewhat. It really didn't feel like he was going on a first date at all. It felt more like he'd known her for years, and that their meeting that evening was just one of many already gone by. He was slightly nervous still; but the nerves in question were gilt-toned, golden.

He wondered if she herself were up yet. He wondered how she was feeling, nervous, excited? He wondered if perhaps she had the same sense that though they'd only met twice, only spoken twice, and very briefly – that somehow, in some liminal, uncanny way, they knew each other, had known each other from long before. The idea of Metempsychosis had never seemed plausible as a metaphysical proposition to him. But now, with this mildly magical perception, it made more sense. Perhaps he and Farida had known each other in a previous life, their souls' journeys rendering them paramours over and over and over again, infinitely recurring? He liked the idea.

*

Farida woke from her dream in a sweat. Quickly, she recounted it to herself, before the memory of it dispersed.

She was on a boat, a large white cruise liner, heading to the North Pole. She was playing cards with a group of Eskimos in one of the recreation areas of that cruise liner. They were playing poker, and though she couldn't now remember a single hand, by the looks of the chips stacked in front of her, she had been winning. Then, in the blink of an eye, she was standing by the rail of the uppermost deck, overlooking a vast white desert of ice and snow. She wasn't overly cold, which was strange in this region. The next moment she had disembarked and was walking without undue effort across the whiteness. Silence reigned, everywhere. And in the dream, she knew it to be the long, slow silence she'd always wished for; the silence of the heart, the heart slaked, sated. Not a sound, then. In the distance, she spotted a polar bear, seemingly a mother, perambulating with her cubs. The she-bear beamed at her, their eyes meeting, as though they'd been doing so for centuries. And just as she felt herself on the verge of uttering a word, she woke up, opened her eyes, sweating. She'd forgotten to turn the AC on the night before, so her body was moist and clammy. She had almost leapt into the shower.

At the age of thirty-four, a Moroccan immigrant and a divorcée, perhaps she had no right to roam so freely in her mind. But roam she did, while munching her breakfast, comprising two pieces of crispy brown toast layered with cream cheese and strawberry jam, the expensive French kind. Her coffee, though, was instant; she'd not the patience for real, bona fide coffee beans, and anyway she wasn't a snob about the drink.

Her cigarettes were sumptuous; she smoked a long, extra-slim kind, packaged in boxes with a violet-purple sheen. Looking at the glamorous colour, she admitted to herself that, yes, it was an overtly gendered shade, there to snag the desirous eyes of the weaker, fairer sex; weaker: supposedly. But then, no, weaker in fact. She was stupid to smoke, and not just for health reasons. Cigarettes were an added expense, especially since the recently imposed VAT. For all the absence of income tax there in Dubai, some of that money was quite bounteously recouped with other, smaller taxes by the wayside! It was true that she only smoked five or six cigarettes per day – one with her morning coffee, usually, one after each meal, and a couple in the interstices of her daily routine. That wasn't too much, after all. So, like most things in life, the case could be argued either way. She should have been a lawyer! She would have been, with the right opportunity at the time. But no, she'd been swindled into an early, disastrous marriage. That divorce had been the bad and menacing moulder of her life. She resolved to desist with these detrimental thoughts, because of the sacredness of the day.

So, Eid. It was great to be able to eat and drink again during the saner hours of the day; smoking, though, she hadn't stopped during her fasting over the Ramadan, which had just come into its acme this Eid-morning. She liked to think that in this matter the exception proved the rule. It was as if by continuing to smoke during daylight hours, while duly abstaining from food or drink, the cigarettes smoked were a message to the Deity that she just could not quite be the purified person that He demanded her to be. Rather than a transgression, it was actually (as she formulated it to herself) even more of a fierce act of devotion, of humility. She said to herself, quite simply, that God would understand the paradox! If it made some kind of sense to her, then it was already resumed in the mind of God, and nothing was or ever could be greater than Him.

But perhaps her faux pas, committed with full awareness, and her theorising were indeed a failing – and worse, a failing doubled, for being justified, to boot, by the sophistry of a waylaid mind? She should have been a lawyer! But then, it was good she worked in cosmetics, because thinking too much was of course a drag, though in her own untutored way, she had a gift for it. The thought of Saeed striding towards her with a dopey smile on his face, in his pristine white *kandura* beneath the electric sun, now softened the walls of her mind.

'Fortuna's Wheel,' she thought. It was, as she understood it, an image of fate or of chance that derived from the Renaissance, centuries ago in the West. She only knew the term because it was something Hala had mentioned once or twice, bubbling with excitement at the idea of ideas as she always was. God, she was such a clever girl! Fortuna's Wheel was supposed to mean the way your life was gifted or rutted by destiny. Farida liked the idea, picturing to herself a kind of roulette table. She'd never seen a roulette table in person, never having been to a casino, though there were many in Morocco. But she'd seen them in the movies, and it piqued her to think that later that day she'd have her own chance to gamble on destiny! But then she mocked herself mentally; and, more seriously, berated herself for picturing such a forbidden image on this day of all days: Eid!

She hadn't asked Hala anything about her brother since he'd invited her for coffee, and she'd accepted. Twice she'd thought of texting her, but twice she'd stopped herself. She'd gathered from snippets of Hala's conversation over the years that her brother was a cerebral man, a bookworm. He didn't look like one, though; he looked good. He had these deep-set almond-coloured eyes, streaked by a kind of green. He had a way of gazing that only enhanced the feeling she got, when looking directly at him, that behind those eyes were abysses of thinking and feeling, wide and sublime, like grand canyons. He was, in short, supposed to be deep.

Her date was at four that afternoon. It was now late morning. She'd some shopping to do. She set off from her small studio apartment, walking a mile or so in the garish heat to the metro station. She was headed for the Mall, having decided recently that she needed a new watch. Her current one only functioned intermittently, and had been given to her by her mother well over a decade earlier, while she was still living in Morocco, working as a private beautician. So, it was time to refresh the clock; and there were some sales on at the Mall, for Eid. Naturally, she planned to benefit from them – she'd be mad not to. Having a date, her first real date in at least four years, certainly did not mean that the routine needs and responsibilities of daily life suddenly stopped being pertinent! It was a coffee, only a coffee.

As she now figured it, as she entered the women and children's compartment of the train, she'd have time to return, then shower again, and get ready to head off to the meeting point Saeed had suggested.

He wasn't picking her up by car; no, thankfully he hadn't had the gumption to suggest that. She'd Googled the meeting place, though; it was a bistro-bar on the second floor of a five-star hotel in the Jumeira area. Why Saeed had chosen a sports bar, she couldn't fathom. But it was a coffee, only a coffee; and, perhaps, a thrilling, novel conversation with a handsome, brainy man.

She had nothing to lose.

Only the risk of crushed hope perhaps; and a wearier heart.

X

A rush of cool, chilling air brushed against Saeed's skin, as the door to the indoor section of the café swung open to let some customers through. Edouard was in the midst of pulling the door closed when Saeed, putting up a plaintive hand for attention, asked if they might keep it open, because the resulting draught cooled them in this afternoon heat.

'Yes, sir,' Edouard answered, 'but then it only heats up the indoors, by the same token. I'm afraid we're not permitted.'

'Why are we sitting outdoors anyway?' Farida asked.

'Because I gathered you like to smoke. I do too.'

There was nothing awkward or shy about the way they talked to each other on this, their first date. They seemed to click to each other's wavelength immediately. It was uncanny, but far from unmanning. Perhaps it was their closeness in age? Saeed had been warned by his mother and his aunts to search for a younger woman as his bride. But then, he wasn't thinking of Farida that way – only as someone he might love. A bride was a formula; a lover was a reality, *the* reality.

'You don't want to marry a woman past thirty,' Lamise had warned him. 'She has fixed ideas, and thinks herself something quite special by then. She thinks she is a "somebody".' Saeed had winced at this, but his mother had continued unabated. 'Which is fine of course, if she's not marrying. But a woman in her twenties still, well, she can adapt to any man she's bound to.'

But no, Saeed had the mellow temper of a man who wanted an intellectual equal as his partner. He'd gathered that Farida had not finished her Bachelor's degree. She'd started a law degree, years and years ago, in Morocco. But then there had been the fiasco, as she described it, of a young, failed marriage. He sensed, however, that though she might not have had the formal schooling, by instinct and intuition she was a thinker.

It was an old concern of his, he now explained. It didn't occur to him (which was typical of his absent-mindedness) that this kind of thing might be a touch too much for a first meeting, face to face.

'You see, the "liberal arts" do not necessarily make one more humane, more liberal. While it is perfectly possible for humane study to make a man, or a woman, more humane, that enlightening process is only a potentiality, a possibility. I guarantee you that your average unschooled man or woman – in some rustic Indian village, say – he or she knows in their bones what it is to be a human being, and a *humane* being at that, as much as the schooled. If he or she loves, hates, feels envy and doubt, recollects, regrets, has desires and needs; if he or she has children, to whom they are unconditionally devoted – well, that person just knows the whole story of being, and of being human.'

Farida was close to being smitten. There was nothing forced about his words, for all their being intellectual. Heavy-duty, no doubt, for a first coffee-date; but refreshing. Like so few men in her life, and from the get-go, he engaged the better part of her. Listening to him was a challenge, and a delight.

'Of course, they might not be articulate about it,' he continued. 'They couldn't write you an essay explaining the insights they live by. But ultimately, it all comes to the same thing.'

It was true, of course. But how could a man who had seen the world, and so evidently had a stellar brain – an Arab man, at that – be modest as well? Were there men like that? There? Then? Of course, there might be; but then, why would it fall to her to have the lucky encounter? Something was off. Something was definitely off. The almonds of his eyes, though, were melting in her own. She couldn't help but wonder? Wonder who this man in fact was, and why he should have chanced into her life like this? He continued to regale her with his warm insights, and she, beside herself, continued intent. And then, peering at her with a querulous, bashful smile, so like a child, he now took the metaphorical foot off the pedal. He was talking too much?

Resting her chin on her right hand, leaning in over across the small round table, still riveted, Farida said:

'No. Not at all. What you say makes sense. A lot of sense. To be honest, I didn't expect this.'

'What?'

'I knew you were a bookish man. Hala always talks about you when she's at the salon. But I assumed... I'd just assumed, Hala's brother or not, you'd be, well, snootier.'

'Wait. You'll see. I can be an elitist too, you know!'

She giggled, and ran a finger through a long stray hair, brushing it round an ear beneath the half-fallen hijab. Her smile was a missile.

'Now that you mention it, elitism – I mean, believing in standards, and ultimately, in excellence in whatever field, cosmetics included – elitism does not necessarily have to be undemocratic. In today's world, especially. Maybe the more conservative temperaments in the contemporary climate are the last bastion left, the last stand, protecting a world of value from slipping away and becoming dispersed, forever. And not just for themselves and their cohorts in some metaphorical ivory tower, but for all of us.'

That made sense, as well. It wasn't so much that he was right, which he was, in her humble view at least; it was the impassioned way he spoke, full of knowledge, but not cold with it – no, he was full of heat, like a painter of some sort, dipping his brush in his palette and swishing brushstrokes onto her heart. But she was doing her best to stay steady.

She now asked him why he'd returned to Dubai, then? Surely the UK – where he'd already had a foot in the door – was a more propitious place for a man of culture?

'I love this place. I just love it. It's my true and final alma mater. It's like an old friend, one you've grown up with. You might never see them for decades, but later in life, when you meet again, you can almost start up the same conversation from where you left off. Yes, I have seen some of the rest of the world. And Dubai is still young, yes. But home is home.'

Feeling more emboldened, knowing it was a risk, Farida now said:

'And why is it you've never married, Saeed?'

Saeed breathed deeply, exhaled.

'I've never met anyone who'd suit a man like me. And then, of course, by the time you get to my age, you're stuck, rigid, fixed the way you are. I suppose in some ways I'm married to my work, and to my projects. And, well, I'm not sure there's a woman out there who'd put up with that.'

Edouard now opened the door again, and left it wide open.

'Never mind, sir,' he said to Saeed. 'It's not so hot anymore. My manager gave the OK.'

Saeed thanked the tall, skinny Ugandan man.

'By the way, wasn't your brother, that budding journalist – wasn't he going to contact me?'

Edouard beamed. It was so gallant of this man to remember; and to go out of his way to remind him.

Farida and Saeed, almost like twins of each other, looked on at the waiter, expectant. They had the same pleasant, confident and confiding feel about them. Edouard, who had a sharp intuition when it came to descrying persons' auras, sensed that these were decent people; not just generous, but innocent.

'He has your card, sir. I don't think he wishes to trouble you on the Eid itself.'

'Nonsense. There's no better time. Besides, I might not feel as generous after the sacral season!'

'I will tell him, sir.'

When the waiter was gone, Farida asked what that was all about, and Saeed explained.

'The young chap's a writer, I gathered the other day. It behoves one to pay it forward. When you get to a certain height, on whatever ladder, I think it's important to lend a hand to those still at a lower stage of the climb. I've always believed that.'

Naturally, she admired the sentiment; it was not laden with the kind of inbred and serpentine venality so typical in the more ambitious Arab men she'd come to know in her life. Those she'd met over the years, at least those on the up-and-up, were in fact just like many of the Arab women she knew. A beauty salon was the perfect place to watch and gauge the phenomena of creeping, mutually infected envy; it infested so many of her clients, robed regally at times, sure, but nonetheless with the spiritual qualities of amoebae. That was why, she now said, Hala was a jewel, and why she loved her so much.

And the feeling was mutual, Saeed replied. But her comment about 'Arabs' was a touch 'Orientalist'.

Farida said it might well be; but it was still true.

She beguiled him. He changed the subject.

They chatted for a few more minutes, without any ruffling of the seamless web of mutual admiration forming between them. Edouard returned to their table and placed a large square brownie with a lump of vanilla ice cream between the couple.

Farida said, politely, that they hadn't ordered it. Edouard protested that it was on the house. He wanted to show his appreciation to Saeed, and his lovely friend. So, with thanks, they dug in. Saeed liked the way Farida wolfed her portion down in a few bites, eschewing false delicacy. She was her own person.

Saeed had done much of the talking, as they'd communed in slow, amorous, lowered tones, waiting for the sunset – but sunrise, or better, dawn, was the truer modality in both. The humidity and the heat of Dubai was an icicle compared to their now-young, newly bit and sudden hearts, lit and glowing like reviving embers.

It was now well past six o'clock in the evening. Saeed offered to drop Farida off back home, but she declined, reminding him that she had her own car. His absent-mindedness was becoming endearing.

Besides, she wanted to be by herself, to reflect and meditate. She wanted to weigh the new experience in the balance of her heart and mind, undistracted.

'Thank you, Saeed. I had fun. I learnt a lot.' She smiled as she stood there, in her black robe lined by golden thread, worn above blue jeans and a white shirt, and her dimples showed.

'Could we... could we do this again sometime?'

Farida nodded, shyly; for the first time, shyly.

As they were leaving the small Parisian-style bistro-bar, Saeed spotted Rachel sat with a couple who looked Lebanese. He decided, quickly, not to approach; he didn't want to interrupt their evening, or his own, sepia-toned thoughts. But a small part of him gladdened at the idea that Rachel might have now made this place a regular haunt.

Bassam was saying to his wife, May, and to Rachel:

'This is quite a place. Oliver mentioned it once, I think, but I've never been.'

'Well, I only discovered it the other day myself,' said Rachel.

'It's a shame Oliver couldn't make it. I wanted to pick his brain about something, an investment.'

His wife, May, now interjected:

'Oh Bassam! Let's not talk business today! Please!'

To which the Lebanese smiled, roundly. Rachel told them, yet again, about how time was money, and then the trio chuckled. That was Dubai, for some people at least.

Bassam spotted a man, handsome in a dopey kind of way, dressed in a pristine white *kandura*, who seemed to be leaving the place. He pointed at him and said:

'That, too, is Dubai. Traditional garb like that, on the Eid, in a bar!'

Rachel looked round, but failed to recognise the man, whose parting, disappearing back was all she could see.

As the man in the *kandura* made his exit he was brushed by a burly African young man entering the place, out of breath, his eyes wide, clearly on tenterhooks. Rachel watched him, gently amused, as he rushed at one of the waiters on the other side of the bistro-bar. In cahoots, they seemed to be discussing something of urgency. She watched the thickset, younger-seeming man slap his right hand against his right thigh while slamming his right foot down. He was frustrated by something. The older man, the waiter (they could have been brothers!) seemed to be calming the younger, who pursed his lips and seemed now close to acquiescence. Whatever it was that had him in such a hot fury could wait. Rachel continued to watch the two men, who looked like puppets, while Bassam and May were busy perusing the menu. The younger, thickset one now placed a chunky sheaf of ruffled papers onto the bar in a huff, while the older man still made pacifying motions with his hand – seemingly still in the act of reasoning with the flustered one. The latter now started to frantically search in his pockets, eventually pulling out what looked like a business card. The elder now smiled, almost maternally on the younger. He motioned to the bartender to get the fellow a pint of beer, and then came over to their table to take their order. Bassam looked up from the menu, as did May. Rachel smiled at them, gesturing them to go ahead. They ordered their meal, and then she did, too. She opted for the same meal which she'd first tasted only the other day, when introduced to the place by Saeed – Atlantic cod on a bed of risotto flavoured by saffron.

When at last, after some dithering, they parted, Saeed watched Farida's small car speed off, looking after it with the glory and the agony of new, richer life simmering in his eyes. He had a metaphoric lump in his throat. He sat in his car's driver's seat now, motionless.

A good five minutes later, he exhaled, started the ignition and drove off. But as he emerged from the upward ramp of the parking lot (which was free today!) he nearly bumped into a cab, almost smacking into it side-on. The Pakistani cab driver honked his horn, vigorously. Saeed watched the driver's thick mouth opening and closing wildly, as he no doubt vented his spleen in a stream of expletives.

Truth be told, though, Hakim had been a touch touchy all day. To have to work in his cab, even a different shift, on the sacred day of Eid! Yes, Vinod had agreed to exchange shifts, because Hakim had wanted a lie-in on this holiday. But the company was adamant, and the mass of Dubai was on the move that day, especially; so curtailed shifts might hold, but not a complete day off! As Hakim finished his slow litany of cursing, one of his passengers – the Filipino man, who was in the back seat with his wife and child – asked him to calm himself, which he presently did.

'Please do not swear like that,' the man said, 'my boy shouldn't hear such things.'

Hakim peered round and spied Adam, who was clutching Benedict, his toy dinosaur. He smiled at the young child. Then smiled at Shirley, too.

'A child is a gift of God,' he said. 'I apologise.'

Yes, Hakim said to himself, such obscenities just wouldn't do for a statesman among cabbies!

Ricardo thanked God the Father, God the Son, and God the Holy Spirit.

Adam now said, while wagging the arm of his toy dinosaur:

'Benedict is hungry, Mummy.'

Shirley promised they'd be home soon.

Roughly fifteen minutes later, when Saeed had made it back to his own home, he still felt elated, lit like a firework. Just as he entered the door of their small camel-coloured villa, his phone tinkled; a text message.

He opened it and read.

Acknowledgments

This book would and could not have been written without the companionship of my wife, Faten Yaacoub. From its original conception her filmic mind triggered, spurred then ratified the progress of my writing this tale. Dubai has been our shared home now for over two years.

Bookclub and writers' circle notes for all the Fairlight Moderns can be found at
www.fairlightmoderns.com

Share your thoughts about the book with **#MinutesMiracleCity**

Also in the Fairlight Moderns series

More coming soon.

SOPHIE VAN LLEWYN

Bottled Goods

*Longlisted for The Women's Prize for Fiction 2019,
People's Book Prize for Fiction 2018 and The Republic
of Consciousness Prize 2019*

When Alina's brother-in-law defects to the West,
she and her husband become persons of interest to
the secret services and both of their careers come
grinding to a halt.

As the strain takes its toll on their marriage,
Alina turns to her aunt for help – the wife of a
communist leader and a secret practitioner of the
old folk ways.

Set in 1970s communist Romania, this novella-
in-flash draws upon magic realism to weave a
captivating tale of everyday troubles.

*'It is a story to savour, to smile at, to rage against
and to weep over.'*
—Zoe Gilbert, author of *FOLK*

*'Sophie van Llewyn's stunning debut novella
shows us there is no dystopian fiction as frightening as that which draws on history.'* — Christina
Dalcher, author of *VOX*

NIAL GIACOMELLI

The Therapist

'I am levitating above the curvature of the earth. Weightless, unencumbered. Flung like a comet out of the atmosphere to drift eternally along the firmament.'

In this bittersweet and hauntingly surreal tale, a couple finds the distance between them mirrored in a strange epidemic sweeping the globe. Little by little, each victim becomes transparent, their heart beating behind a visible rib cage, an intricate network of nerves left hanging in mid-air. Finally, the victims disappear entirely, never to be seen again.

'I dreamt we were at sea,' she says.

Praise for the *Fairlight Moderns*:

'A delectable compilation of modern novellas from writers all over the globe.'
—The Big Issue

ANTHONY FERNER

Inside the Bone Box

'On a good day at work, the tips of his fingers seemed to tingle with focused energy. They sensed the space, rose, turned through angles, intuited the tissue, felt the consistency of flesh, used just the right degree of delicacy or brutality.'

Nicholas Anderton is a highly respected neurosurgeon at the top of his field. But behind the successful façade all is not well. Tormented by a toxic marriage and haunted by past mistakes, Anderton has been eating to forget. His wife, meanwhile, has turned to drink.

There are sniggers behind closed doors – how can a surgeon be fat? When mistakes are made and his old adversary steps in to take advantage, Anderton knows things are coming to a head…

'A little book that packs a punch far greater than its size.' —The Idle Woman, blogger